REPRISAL

He rode alone but with him he carried always the memory of his father's murder.

A range war, an ambush, a shot in the back . . . his father dead on a dark night in the hills between Blackrock and Morgantown.

It had happened a long time ago but Jim Reno would never rest until he found the killer. Somewhere that man walked the streets, ate, slept, fully confident that he was safe after all these years.

He did not know that his minutes were numbered. He did not know that his victim's son was headed his way, his guns cocked and ready.

More Westerns from SIGNET

– 1 –

Smiling Fugitive

Jim Reno, riding along the bottom of a considerable arroyo, heard the shot smash out of the right forward distance with that thinning flatness made only by a rifle. For a moment he thought he was the target—the natural reaction of a man with something of a price on his head—and his instant response was to crowd his pony against the more abrupt side of the arroyo and sweep it both ways. But nothing showed and no bullet's dust-dimple lifted its telltale shape; and lifting his eyes immediately thereafter to the bald bench he had been paralleling all this afternoon, he found neither marksman nor ravel of gunsmoke. Thus alertly poised he heard the speaking through the sultry silence again.

That moved him. Leaving the saddle he crawled to the rim of the arroyo, and there he saw the whole story in one long survey. A rider fled up the undulating pitches of the bench with every evidence of a mad haste, leaving a banner of dust behind him—the length of that banner showing exactly which creased depression he had started from. Out in the open prairie, about a thousand yards behind him, a horse stood on dropped reins, and slightly aside from the horse a man's body turned over and over on the ground. "Hit bad," mused Reno. Then, because his experience with grief in its multifold forms had taught him never to forget himself, he added: "And if he dies, here I am right on the premises to be accused of doing it." Looking back to the bench, he watched the ambusher at last curl about a dun knob and vanish.

"I'm a sucker if I go out there," he grumbled. "Nothing but grief comes to the good Samaritan." Then he turned about and his eyes, sharp blue against the swept smoothness of a bronze skin, quested the back trail. As far as he could see, which was about three miles, there was only emptiness—good enough indication that his recent maneuvering in the pocketed country had thrown the posse temporarily off his scent. He had, he supposed, a three-hour lead; and with that decided, he slid back to his pony and rose out of the arroyo. Aiming for the fallen one, he shook his head with a mild feeling of contempt for his own weakness.

"Probably get shot for my pains," he observed. "Posse behind, fellow with a rifle up on the bench, and this poor devil dyin' out there—him no doubt thinkin' I'm the one that got him."

He did, then, a characteristic thing. He grinned, and the grin lightened the assured and rather hard cast of his features. The pressed severity of his mouth was released, small weather-wrinkles deepened about the eyes, and at once a touch of ironic, uncaring recklessness lay revealed. Three hundred feet from the prone hand, he checked in, straightening his tall flat torso. The fellow showed some sign of life. One hand reached outward. A dark and pointed face became distinct.

"Easy," called Reno. "I didn't dry-gulch you."

A surprisingly strong voice came out of the man. "I know that. Come on up."

Reno crossed the interval and slipped to the ground, immediately feeling a profound pity. Here was a young magnificently set-up body, long and leanly powerful. But it was shattered now beyond repair. There wasn't any hope; the man was going out. A telltale sweat streaked the dark skin and a grayish pallor mottled it. Now and then one long leg lifted from a reflex of pain. All that remained strongly alive were the eyes. The light that came out of them was vital, almost fiercely intense.

"Take care of yourself," said the man. "Look and see if—if he's still in sight."

"No. He pulled out after the second shot. Now, old trapper, we've got to do something in a hurry. I'll lift you—"

6

But the man shook his head, a slow, grim gesture of defeat. "Leave me alone. I'd fall to pieces."

"You're sure of that?" asked Reno, profoundly stirred. He had seen men die before—often enough in fact to have developed that deep and quiet sense of fatalism that colored all his thoughts and sometimes made him seem callous to suffering. But here was a man dying as a man ought to die—without fear and without crying. The bright black glance was actually defiant. It was hard to see such fine courage wasted.

"You're a stranger," grunted the man.

"Yes. Anything I can do?"

"If you're no fool, you'll never stop till this cursed country is behind you," said the man with heavy bitterness.

"You know who got you?" asked Reno.

"Not sure," the other said with effort. He pressed his lips together and Reno understood he would make no guesses. On impulse he rose and got his canteen and tipped it to the man's lips. Afterwards he took off his hat and shaded the upstaring face.

"Bound anywhere in particular?" asked the fellow.

"If you want a message delivered," said Reno, "I'll carry it."

The fellow's eyes closed. He said rapidly: "Go to Morgantown and find Big Lafe McMurtree. Tell him. Tell him Two-Bits is dead. Tell him—it was a rifle shot."

"That's all?" asked Reno.

"Take my gun with you. Give it to him."

"Nothing else?" pressed Reno. "No information as to who it might have been?"

A great change appeared to shake the prone fellow. All muscular movement became faint. His voice dropped to a faint, rumbling pitch. And with his eyes still closed he said: "No, nothing. That's all."

Reno's deep sympathy moved him to reach out and grip the other's arm. And he said something then he never would have said to another person. "When you cross the Jordan ferry, my friend, the valley beyond will be green with grass and freshly watered. It'll be

7

a pleasant place to camp. Is there no woman you'll want to send a word to?"

"Me?" muttered the other. "A McMurtree? What woman cares for that black tribe? There's only one in all the hills to grieve. She shouldn't, for we've hurt her ever since she was a kid. But she'll think kindly of me long after the rest have forgotten."

"Open your mouth," said Reno, tipping the canteen.

But there was no obeying gesture and Reno, looking down with a close curiosity, saw the other's lids slowly relax and creep partially open. He knew then, even before he laid his hand across that broad chest, what the answer was—the fellow had drifted on.

Rising slowly, Reno replaced the canteen and reached for his cigarette tobacco. Along the lean jaws appeared a sudden tightness, and the rest of his features took sharper and harder form—the unconscious reaction of a man who hated injustice; for at twenty-seven, with rather bitter and rough-and-tumble experience to draw from, he still possessed the instinctive fighter's sense of sureness and he still glowed with hot anger when cruelty and oppression and treachery came within his view.

"Another good hand ridin' into the sunset too soon," he muttered.

Lifting his eyes then, he saw that sunset was not far away, and it reminded him of the fact that he was losing the good minutes. He could do nothing more here. His position was dangerous, his promise to the dead man laid him wide open to further uncertainty. Nor could he undertake to move the fellow to the nearest town. That chore, he realized, would be done by the posse now undoubtedly closing up. What he had to do in short order was to put the miles behind him and to watch with an increasing vigilance. For it became plainer each moment that he stood a strong chance of being accused of this killing.

Reaching down, he got the other man's gun—a .45 with a worn grip that had a star and crescent inlay of mother-of-pearl—and stowed it in a saddlebag. Then he

8

swung up and lined out to the eastward at a strong canter. Another rear glance showed a clear trail.

"But," he reflected soberly, "this whole business is unfortunate for me. I'm a stranger and I'm mixed up in something that probably has a lot of strings tied to it. This range is no different than any other. Whoever wanted that fellow dead will move a lot of dirt to put the job on me. I expect to be challenged any time."

When the sun fell beneath the earth he was a good eight miles off in the depths of a land that ran west and south without visible break—a free and open range good to the rider's eye. To the north the tawny bench still paralleled him, increasing in ruggedness and backed up by a considerable range of hills that swung forward from the distance. Just as dusk fell he looked behind again and thought he made out the posse far off. Then darkness came with a rush and he laid the sandy miles beneath him, one by one. By degrees the bench began to curve away, and he followed along that bend with the general belief that the town he sought, which was Blackrock, stood somewhere ahead with one face showing to the prairie and the other confronting the hills. Around the bend he saw it in the shape of crystal-pointed lights all aglitter across the flats; and about eight o'clock he entered the narrow central street of a range town. A double row of locusts ran the length of the street, increasing the shadows of the buildings. A saloon blazed brilliantly nearby, men walked indolently beneath the second-story porch roofs, there was the sound of guitar and fiddle somewhere. Coming upon a water trough, Jim Reno let his pony drink sparingly, then rode into the adjacent stable's runway. When he dismounted a hostler advanced from the darkness within.

"Grain him," said Reno, "but keep the saddle on him."

The hostler's face came closer and was thin and inquisitive. "Keep the saddle on?" he said.

"Yes," replied Reno shortly, and turned away. He knew that so simple an order exposed his hand, and he knew too that the news would spread. All these towns were alike, alert and suspicious, weighing strangers in the light of local politics. But he could hope for nothing better, nor could any other man on the run. Such deliberate plans as he had laid were worthless now, made so by the death of that rider on the prairie, and he could only guide himself from one uncertain situation to another. Understanding this, he strolled into a restaurant and ordered a meal.

"Only thing I'm sure of," he reflected over his eggs and bacon, "is that nobody will recognize me. Nobody."

Afterwards he went back to the street, fashioning a cigarette in the shadows. Half a dozen townsmen sat on the porch steps to his immediate right and talked in drawling syllables; the casual strollers drifted in and out of the saloon across the way. But as he paused in his tracks, debating with himself, he noticed one man walk from that saloon with an air of purpose and come across. He passed Reno at arm's distance, not seeing him; and he went straight to the stable, there turning in. It meant nothing, it meant anything; Reno held his place, on guard. A little later the man emerged from the stable and strode back to the saloon.

"Thought so," said Reno to himself, and dragged a deep draught of smoke through his mouth. He had wondered about making his appearance in the saloon, but he realized now that it was a necessary step. Somebody was showing a curiosity he had to satisfy. "I've got," he reflected, "about an hour. Posse will be here then." So considering, he went over and shouldered through the swinging doors. At the bar he ordered his whisky and, dawdling against the bar, he studied the place through the plate glass mirror behind it.

It was comfortably filled, this room. Smoke hung thickly from the ceiling like ropes of moss and riders tramped around with the leisurely restlessness that rises from a full stomach and a free night. A half-dozen poker tables were in full blast. Two floormen moved swiftly through the crowd and somebody called rather sharply: "Three sevens will take this pot." Reno drank and laid his glass down.

10

"Stranger?" asked the barkeep, looking closely at Reno.

"Never saw me before?" countered Reno.

"No-o."

"Must be a stranger then," said Reno, eyes going back to the mirror. He saw something reflected from a far corner of the room. Over there three men stood against a wall and looked at him with more than casual attention. One of them—tall and broad and beyond the middle of life—bent his head and spoke briefly to the fellow at his left hand. That was all. The trio split and the addressed party strolled from the place. Reno paid his bill thoughtfully and turned out. Past the doors he sidestepped to get away from the light and went on down the walk.

"If I'm going to get clear of Blackrock," he thought, "it had better be now. Those men showed something more than idle curiosity. Might have expected it."

He drew up with a swift, defensive motion. A slim figure drifted away from a dark wall, wheeled across his path, and spoke with a softness and a casualness infinitely deceptive. "No offense, but there's somebody as wants to talk to you."

"I don't know anybody here," parried Reno.

"Would that make any difference?" asked the other.

"If he wanted to talk to me bad enough—I guess not," admitted Reno.

"That's it," said the other gently.

But Reno was exploring his chances and so he went on. "I'm not on anybody's payroll. Why should I take orders?"

"This man," answered the other, "is accustomed to having his way." And then a touch of cold insistence came into the words. "Anyhow, your horse probably won't be ready for you short of another ten-fifteen minutes."

"I wondered about that," remarked Reno. "All right. Lead the way."

The man turned, cut into an alley beside the saloon. Trailing down this utter gloom, Reno swung around

11

a corner and stumbled through the clutter of boxes and trash. The man halted, tapped lightly on a door, and opened it. "Go ahead," he said, and Reno stepped into a room that was, he immediately recognized, directly behind the bar. All the sounds of the crowd came through in muted proportions. The messenger closed the door.

There were three men—that messenger, the tall and heavy fellow Reno had noticed before, and another whose square and bold and inordinately hard face had a look of brusque cruelty. Reno knew the types of men who rode the prairie, and his weighing glance told him all he wished to know about this particular hand. Straight or crooked, the fellow was a driver and a killer. He weighed around two hundred pounds, his hips and legs were powerful after the fashion of a bronc buster. His torso was thin at the flanks and broadened again at the shoulders. He had long arms, the hands of which were oddly tapered and supple—good hands for a gun, Reno instantly thought. But it was the face that dominated Reno's attention—that harsh, blackened face with the pressed mouth, the flattened cheekbones, and the drilling, blinkless eyes as bleak as the jet black hair showing beneath the man's hat.

All this he gathered at a glance. But he had been long enough at it to draw a dry comment from the older man in the room, who said shortly: "You're lookin' at my foreman, Hale Wolfert."

Reno swung his glance over to this one—quite a big man with a small, nut-shaped head on which were a series of sly and sharp Yankee features. His hair was white and he was perhaps better than sixty. Reno asked a sudden question. "Then who are you?"

"Peter Vilas," said the man, and seemed to watch for something definite to show on Reno's cheeks. Catching no reaction, he added another dry observation: "I own some of the prairie."

"What of it?" challenged Reno.

Vilas chuckled and looked at his foreman. "Comes to the point, don't he, Hale?"

But Wolfert neither answered nor moved. His eyes

12

clung steadily to Reno and a scowling disfavor appeared to collect in them.

Vilas spoke abruptly to the third man, the one who had brought Reno to this room. "That's all, George." And George slipped quietly through the door. Vilas went on. "You were probably on your way straight through Blackrock, wasn't you?"

"What makes you think so?" asked Reno.

"Left your horse saddled in the stable."

"I wondered who was interested enough to go look," observed Reno.

Vilas expelled that humorless fragment of a chuckle again. "You're a sharp boy. Any name?"

"Reno—Jim Reno."

"It will do as good as any," said Vilas shrewdly. "Now, Reno, I need a favor done. I was thinking you'd do it."

"Why?"

"Because," said Vilas pointedly, "I can do you one."

"Maybe—maybe not," was Reno's noncommittal answer.

"Oh yes. I can keep you from falling into the hands of the sheriff. Is that a good guess or ain't it?"

"What's the favor you need?" parried Reno.

"I want a message delivered. Nothing more."

Hale Wolfert suddenly came out of his long silence. "I don't think you better use him, Pete."

"Why not?" demanded Vilas.

"I don't believe you better."

"Know anything about him?"

"No," said Wolfert.

"Then what's your objection?"

Hale Wolfert said emotionlessly: "I don't like the looks of him."

Quiet came to the room, and Reno stood there with the full force of both men's prying inspections beating on him. Vilas' little head came forward and his sly face became deeply thoughtful. But he said finally: "I can judge a man as well as you, Hale. He'll do. It's no odds anyway."

13

Wolfert shrugged his shoulders, and Vilas turned to Reno again. "How about it?"

"I see the point," drawled Reno. "All right. What message and where to?"

"Do you know anything about this country?" asked Vilas.

Reno remained thoughtfully still a moment, then said, "No," with a certain touch of reserve. It brought from Wolfert a more relentless, saturnine attention, and Vilas seemed to check his ready talk. But after a while he nodded and spoke again.

"Well, it's no country for invalids, Reno. I wouldn't send you out and not tell you that. Up in those black hills is a crowd of men that hate the sight of the prairie and everything that walks on the prairie. There's a little joint up there called Morgantown. Seventeen miles away. In the last forty years I do not recall a Morgantown man ever coming to Blackrock. As for the other way around, a Blackrock man couldn't get to Morgantown if he wanted. That's where I want you to take the message."

A long silence fell across the room. Reno studied the other two with an impassiveness that concealed a mask for one thought after another flashing through his brain. The lamp on the table cut long angles beneath his eyes, slanted across the swept bronze of his cheeks. "So," he said at last, "I'm the sucker."

"I was waitin' for that," admitted Vilas with a show of candidness. "But I'm not playin' you for a sucker. It's an out-and-out proposition. You're not takin' anybody's place and you're not inheritin' anything. I can't get a Blackrock man up there without havin' him shot off the road. You're a stranger. You'll make it."

"Who's this message to?"

"I want you to go find Big Lafe McMurtree," said Vilas slowly.

Jim Reno looked down to the table, ran his hand idly across it. "How'll I find him?"

There was no immediate answer, and when he raised his head he saw Vilas staring at Wolfert with an air of suppressed, ironic amusement. "Well," said Vilas, "you'll

14

have no trouble about that. He'll find you. Consider that settled."

"What's the message?"

For reply Vilas turned to the desk and pulled up a chair. He got out a pencil and a piece of paper and for some moments his rawboned fist labored across the paper. He evidently had some trouble in phrasing the note, for he paused now and then to stare at the table or twirl the pencil between his fingers. When he had finished he handed the paper to Reno. "Nothing secret about it. Look at it for yourself."

Reno read this:

> McMurtree: The cattlemen of Blackrock range consider that the long war between hill and prairie has gone far enough. We will countenance no more raids on our beef. Speaking for myself, if this goes on longer I will bring a full party to Morgantown and burn it. Suggest you arrange a meeting with me to settle this Sunday. I am willing to ride anywhere along the base of Drum Peak to talk it out with you. P. Vilas.

"I'll make no friends up there, bringing this," observed Reno.

"There's always some small danger in everything," admitted Vilas. "I didn't say this was shy of possible trouble."

"Supposin' I say no?"

Vilas leaned back and met Reno's glance squarely. "You don't want to meet the sheriff, do you?"

"Thought that was the proper answer," said Reno, "but I wanted to get it straight. All right. Am I supposed to bring back an answer?"

"Answer?" asked Vilas as if he had never thought of it. "Well, now. Well, if there's such a thing as an answer bring it back."

15

"All right," decided Reno, and put the note in his pocket.

"The Morgantown-Blackrock road runs due north of the stable," said Vilas. "Get on your way. I'll see the sheriff, but I don't want him to find you in town."

Reno turned to the back doorway and had his hand on the knob when Hale Wolfert said curtly: "Wait a minute, you." And when he turned around he found the foreman looking at Vilas with a stubborn displeasure.

"Pete," said Wolfert, "think this over before you let him go. I don't like his looks. If he gums up the works where will we be?"

Vilas rose from the table. "What works will he gum up, Hale?" he asked smoothly. "The proposition is plain and above-board, ain't it? Ain't it?"

Wolfert muttered a sound of disgust and pivoted on his heels. Next moment he passed through the inner door to the barroom.

Reno let himself out the back way without further delay, walked to the nearest alley, and paused there. But as he stood watchful and alert in the deep dark, he suddenly changed his mind about using that alley, and instead cruised on until another presented itself. This he followed as far as the street. Then, pressing along the walk to an obscure area where locust and porch created a profound pool of blackness, he started to cross over to the stable. But he never took a step into the roadway. For, poised on the edge of the boards, he heard the cantering drum of a considerable party coming out of the prairie. He stepped back, flattening against the building wall, alert to the quick turn of events. And from that position he saw a dozen riders come down the street double file. As the first building lights reached out to touch them he recognized the sheriff's party.

With all the assurance given him by Peter Vilas, he felt no ease. The same old promptings of self-defense that had carried him so far through his riding years flashed along his nerves now, and his attention began to drift itself toward one point of escape and another. Meanwhile the sheriff's party passed and nosed in at the

16

hitch rack; and looking that way he distinctly saw Hale Wolfert come through the glare of the saloon doors, step aside from the oncoming posse members, and afterwards go rapidly across the street. Something about that maneuver further warned Reno to sudden action, and acting on it he walked straight over to the stable and into it. The hostler stood in the runway, barring his path.

"I'm going out," said Reno abruptly, reaching for his money. "Where's the pony?"

The hostler's answer was reluctant, defensive. "I've had orders."

"Sure. Well, that's over with. Where's the horse?"

"I ain't got any contrary orders," insisted the hostler.

Reno's reply was to reach out and seize the man by the shoulder and spin him around. "This is not your fight, brother, and it will do you no good to get your head busted in it. Where's that horse?"

"Left end stall," grumbled the man.

Reno went past him on the run, reached the stall, and turned into it. He was in the saddle and swinging through the rear doorway when the hostler cried out angrily: "I hope you get your liver blasted out—!"

It was the talk of an angered man yet Reno, cool and taut, heard in it the suggestion of something about to happen—something the hostler knew surely. It prompted him to bend far over against the saddle, and he went out the rear way, across the baked corral area and through a wide gate. Somebody rose up on his flank. As he saw the body rearing up, he slashed the pony with his spurs and sent his hand toward his holster. The blackness bloomed with a sharp crease of light and a deep roar swelled the night. Marking that point, Reno let go with his shots, throwing them down recklessly as he paced away into the open. There was one more reply and then a silence. Over behind that row of buildings—in the street—men began shouting, but the sound soon faded as Reno cleared Blackrock, struck the ruts of a northward road, and faded down it. He was, he knew, in the clear. There would be no pursuit. The ambusher

17

was alone and could not afford to follow. A mile onward he lessened the gait and relaxed.

"Didn't hit him," he said to himself. "But he fell to keep from bein' hit. Wolfert, no doubt about it. He knows something about me Vilas didn't. Yet it don't seem possible he could have recognized me."

Overhead the velvet of the sky was awash with a diamond stream of starlight. In the immediate foreground the bench and the range behind that bench made a barrier without a single flaw of visibility. The ground began rising beneath him, a sharper air poured across the slopes. Sitting easy, he aimed for Morgantown seventeen miles away.

"Nothing Vilas said about this message fooled me. The words of it mean something else, the whole thing is aimed for another purpose. But it will serve my purpose better than if I had planned it deliberately. I'm back. That's the main thing—I'm back to do what is left to be done."

– 2 –

The Deep Hills

There was something deceptive about the rugged land into which he traveled. It seemed to bury him in its depths, yet more than two miles out of Blackrock the first quick tilt of the bench lifted him to a crest from which he caught again the lights of the town. After that the road tackled an increasing grade earnestly, and for long intervals Reno's pony went on at a slogging walk. A bank of fog drifted thickly about him. Beyond that level he was in the pure darkness of tree country and all around him lay the profound stillness and mystery. He had, he realized, put the bench definitely behind him. This was the scarp of that distant range he had seen during the day; but he was not quite done with the prairie, for about a thousand feet above the flats he looked back and saw the glimmer of Blackrock in the distance. Almost immediately thereafter he followed down a long chasm and lost contact with the world. Nothing showed but the dim glitter of the stars above.

"Fine country for hiding," he observed, and then shook his head slowly. "Yet I doubt if I'll have any luck doing it. People in the hills like this are jealous of strangers riding loose. Unless I'm entirely wrong, the sheriff's authority doesn't amount to much beyond this point. But somebody else's authority does. It's always like that."

He went on for better than two hours through the windings of this gorge, the solitude pressing about him like a blanket, feeling the wildness and great isolation of the terrain. And he felt, too, a gradual change. For one thing, the rocky underfooting shifted to a softer

19

soil. For another, the gorge walls began to spread apart; and shortly afterwards he passed what was definitely a side trail running due south along a minor crest of hills. He had not gone far beyond it when he was warned that the trail held other riders.

The warning came abrupt and clear from the hind quarter, in the shape of ponies' feet striking fast and hard on the trail. He had only enough time to crowd his own mount against a side wall of the gorge when they came beating up and by. Crouched there in the saddle, one arm reached across the animal's nostrils, he made out one rearing shadow and another post forward into the gloom. Quick dust rolled out and touched him, and then the rumble of their travel died in the forward distance.

"Twelve or fifteen of them," he said, half aloud. "And they came out of that side trail. Busier than aggravated bees." And afterwards, turning the import of it over and over in his cool mind, he added: "Only a few kinds of business rate that sweat and grunting in the dark. This is the kind of a country I thought it might be."

The cold of this higher altitude cut through his clothing and he risked a cigarette, cupping the match in the crown of his hat, all the while listening for some break in the seeming peace. There was no trust in him. He didn't need the hints of Peter Vilas to put him on guard against these hills; his own primary instincts told him enough. At twenty-seven, Reno was well aware of the fact that any land of night riders would be a land of subterfuge. This was what he pushed into—subterfuge and uncertainty to the point of considerable danger. As for himself, he could play it cautious or he could play it reckless; but the one necessary thing was to tie himself, by one means or another, into the life of these hills. He could accomplish no part of his own secret chore as long as he remained an outlander.

"So," he mused, "I better play it slightly reckless. Seems the surest way." And throwing the cigarette to the earth, he prodded the horse on. "Better play it slightly reckless—and continue the sucker role till it peters out. Nobody will recognize me."

The gorge dissipated itself all at once into a small valley, and as Reno went down the looping grade he was again bathed by a fog thick enough to be stirred by his passage. This, added to the dark, made a blinding element, and he could only let the horse choose its route. Long afterwards—he judged it to be another two miles—he felt the road rise. From a distance a rumbling sound began to lift and reverberate through the night. Presently he got above the fog and caught the faintly etched outline of trees against the blankness of a black sky—which had all the appearance of some quite deep country lying off in that direction. But the road sheered away from it, went directly into the filling rush and mutter of a waterfall. He thought he got the twinkle of a light ahead, but it vanished with an exceeding swiftness, and then the hoofs of his horse woke a series of drumming echoes as it crossed a plank bridge.

Quick as it came about, Reno stiffened in the saddle with all his senses cold and pointed, overtaken by a feeling that nothing happening here would be out of place; and so he was defensively prepared for the instant rapped-out challenge that leaped up from the foreground and struck him across the face.

"Hold up!"

The voice was wholly unfamiliar but the tone of it, full of arrogant certainty, was like a call across the years. In his rough-and-tumble life had been many such challenges, many such curt breaks. He knew the exact meaning of that voice and he knew what to do. His rein arm checked the horse to a slow drifting, and he said casually:

"All right."

"Who is it?" said the voice.

"The name is Reno—Jim Reno."

"Where from?"

"Blackrock."

A little silence ensued, broken finally by a throaty, thrown-out oath. "Either you're lyin' or you've got the nerve of a brass monkey! And where do you figure you're goin' at this hour of the night?"

"Morgantown," said Reno calmly.

He heard then the stir of other men coming afoot from the foreground. The challenging voice was still, but a murmur of back-and-forth talk rose from the rear. A bit of metal clicked. The voice resumed, cynically:

"And I reckon you're just out to get a breath of air—nothin' more."

"No," said Reno crisply, "I've got business up here. Use your head. What in hell else do you suppose would be bringing me into the hills after nightfall?"

"Light that lantern," called the voice, "and let's get a look at this free-spoken customer."

Those other men seemed to be waiting for the order. A match blazed instantly and a lantern's chimney dropped over a clear yellow flame that cut sharp arcs in the black. It came bobbing on and lifted in front of Reno. Looking down at the man behind that lantern, Reno saw a face that reminded him oddly of somebody else—a long and slanting and heavy-featured face. The voice of the spokesman, who still remained beyond view, cut in resonantly: "I don't know you. What's your business up here?"

"I've got a couple of messages for Big Lafe McMurtree. You boys know him?"

"Don't you know him?" parried the other.

"No," said Reno.

"Then," shot back the spokesman with an increase of temper, "you're no Blackrock hand! Better not lie!"

"I didn't say I was a Blackrock hand," returned Reno. "I said I come from there."

"What's the size of these messages?" demanded the spokesman.

"That happens to be none of your business," stated Reno with an even severity.

"Might be some question as to that," grunted the spokesman. But a milder voice came up from the rear. "We better take him to Big Lafe, The'dore."

"Let me handle this," said the spokesman in no pleasant manner.

"Then handle it and quit talkin'," retorted the mild one.

"All right," growled the spokesman, "we'll take him to Big Lafe's."

At the suggestion of command, Reno moved forward with the lantern bearer trudging beside him. A horseman came suddenly abreast on the other side and showed one knife-scarred cheek in the light's thrust. It was, Reno realized, the fellow who had done all the talking. Roan-colored hair showed along the man's temples, and his eyes had a Mongol narrowness to them. Nothing more was said. The lantern bearer abruptly extinguished his light and ran off. Presently the rest of the unseen group came milling into the road, now asaddle—and thus escorted, Reno trotted past a denser point of timber and on toward a glimmering house light. The cavalcade ignored it and curled into a lesser and more abysmally sightless route. It shot upward precipitously, high into a windier world. Somewhere the group turned again and went single file down the barren spine of a ridge. Twenty minutes later the course fell down the side of a canyon where a small creek went rioting between apparently jagged walls that caught the water and threw it into boiling sprays. Reno, trying to establish the windings of this trail in his mind, finally gave up with the feeling that the leader of the party was deliberately complicating the thing, and the feeling became a certainty when they shifted up another stiff slope and came to a momentary halt. One rider trotted on a ways, spoke a subdued phrase, and called back, "All right." The party moved ahead and within a quarter-mile came upon a definite clearing. At the far end sat a house all aglow.

A pack of hounds charged forward in full throat, swirling about the feet of the horses. At the porch a pair of men stepped from the shadows and stood silently alert. The spokesman murmured something indistinct to them and pointed at Reno, who got out of the saddle and moved forward. At the same time a door swung open. Urged by the spokesman's shove, Reno passed into what was the largest room he had ever seen. It was fully three-quarters of the lower floor of this sprawling structure. Above it, reached by a winding staircase, an overhanging gallery ran on four sides; off this gallery opened a series of doors. Reno, sizing it up, thought the place more like a barracks than a ranch house. But this was only a quickly passing reflection, for his attention crossed the room to the huge fireplace beneath the far gallery and fastened itself to the man standing there. The'dore, the spokesman, said bluntly, "There's Big Lafe," and Reno walked on until the welcome heat of the fire touched him and Big Lafe was but an arm's length away.

Big Lafe had been mighty in all his proportions. This was evident at a glance. Even now, obviously in the withering seventies, there was about him a dominating strength and a proud sense of power. His hands were clasped behind him, thus throwing forward a fine, high pair of shoulders. His thews were pronounced, his bones well covered, his chest soundly arched. Well over six feet, he had the tall man's habit of bowing his head to lesser men. He did it now and Reno, who never failed to measure the worth of men about him, saw the light of those ice-blue eyes beneath the shaggy, bushing brows turn intent and sharp. It was a driving sort of inspection, full of insistent challenge and harshness. Yet it was not brutal; nor was that long, contained face antagonistic. Rather the cast of those strong, commanding features was one of discipline and confidence. It was clear to Reno that Big Lafe McMurtree ruled without doubt and had no fear.

The silence held on for a long while and the dozen or so men in the room—all grouped to the rear of Reno—respected it. Big Lafe McMurtree slowly unclasped his hands and swung about to kick a log deeper in the fire. The resultant rise of light flooded across the room. Big Lafe turned back, spoke over Reno's head with a cool abruptness.

"Where'd you find him, The'dore?"

"He came up the Blackrock road like he owned it,"

said The'dore, quickly. "We heard him when he crossed the plank bridge at Garry Creek."

"Seem surprised when you stopped him?"

"No-o," said The'dore with reluctance. "You'd of thought he was doin' us a favor. Said he had a message for you—and wouldn't tell me what it was."

"Wouldn't tell you?" repeated Big Lafe as if that meant something. His cutting glance whipped over to Reno. "What is your name?"

"Reno."

Big Lafe considered it thoughtfully, deeply, then said: "There are no Renos in Blackrock. Where did you come from?"

"I came through Blackrock," said Reno, bearing down on the "through." Then he said: "That is enough for you to know."

"So it's like that?" asked Big Lafe. "Well, what is the message?"

Reno reached into his pocket for the note Vilas had given him and handed it over. McMurtree read what had been written with a sort of aloof calm, folded the paper, and tossed it on the fire. Closely watching for a reaction, Reno found no sign of either anger or excitement on the disciplined cheeks of this old fellow. Big Lafe's glance came back shrewdly to him.

"You know what was in it?"

"Yes."

"There'll be no answer," said Big Lafe casually.

"I judged he expected none."

Big Lafe's eyes narrowed at that. An added sharpness came to his talk. "How much of Vilas' business do you know?"

"None. Never met the man till tonight. But that doesn't stop me from guessin'."

"And he picked you, a stranger, to deliver this?"

"He said no Blackrock man could get this far."

"Then what caused you to tackle a job that might of ended bad for you?"

Reno suddenly grinned. "There was some pressure

in the matter. Vilas agreed to keep the posse off my trail."

Big Lafe shook his head. He said unexpectedly: "You're no crook, my boy."

"Thanks," said Reno, and turned sober. "There's something else I'll have to tell you. This afternoon, ten miles due west of Blackrock, I heard a couple of shots over the hump. When I got up there a fellow was dying on the ground and another fellow riding hellbent into the bench. I could do nothing but give the hit party a little water. Before he died he asked me to find you and to tell you that he was gone. That Two-Bits was gone. And that a rifle got him."

He had expected no great show of emotion, for the short interval in this room had told him clearly that this group of men was bound by an odd quiet and rigid control. Even so, it mildly astonished him that the ensuing moments seemed as blank of sound as the heart of a grave. Not one body behind him shifted, not one breath lifted. As for Big Lafe, the long lips compressed a little and there was some passage of feeling deep behind the eyes. Then the man straightened his fine shoulders.

"How am I to believe this, sir?"

"In my left-hand saddlebag is a gun with a star and crescent inlay he asked me to bring here."

Big Lafe made a slight motion with an arm, at which one of the crowd walked from the room. "Vilas—he knows about this?" demanded the old man.

"I never mentioned it to him."

The hand came back from outside. "No gun in either saddlebag," he called accusingly.

Reno whirled around. "Who's been monkeyin' with my gear? That gun was there."

Big Lafe's voice took on a definite tone of authority. His words cracked across the room. "The'dore, where is the gun?"

The'dore pulled up his head. In the light his face seemed more unprepossessing, more slanting than by the brief rays of the lantern. The scar made a long evil track across one cheek, and those Mongol eyes were narrower

26

than ever. He said a little sullenly: "Nobody has touched that horse since I caught this man. If you want my opinion, the man lies."

"Reno," said Big Lafe slowly, "where else could that gun have gone?"

"I left the horse in Blackrock's stable for half an hour," mused Reno thoughtfully. "I wonder . . ."

"No need to wonder," interrupted Big Lafe, grimly. "It was lifted there—the gun."

"You believe that cock-and-bull story?" The'dore asked of Big Lafe.

"Be silent," snapped Big Lafe. Afterwards he looked to Reno and some part of the rigidness went out of his manner. "I thank you for telling me. It was my nephew you gave the drink of water to. You've done your share, your chore. What next?"

"I'll be ridin' on," said Reno.

"Out of the country?" pressed Big Lafe.

But Reno shook his head. "No. I'll be in the hills for a while."

"Not in these hills," interrupted The'dore. "Nobody rides these hills unless we say so."

"Unless who says so?" challenged Big Lafe.

"Unless you say so," amended The'dore after a long, tight pause. Looking about, Reno saw The'dore's jaw work into lines of balky stubbornness.

Big Lafe said abruptly: "Reno, have you ever been in this part of the country before?"

"No."

"I think," said Big Lafe, "you are lyin'. But we shall soon find out. If you have, there is one pair of eyes in this house that will recognize you—no matter how long you might've been away. Rae!"

The silence settled again. Big Lafe swung half about, facing a door that led back from the lower floor to an inner room. Behind Reno was the utter quiet of men expecting something important to happen. And with this feeling in his bones—the feeling that all his fortunes depended on the next flip of the moment—he stiffened himself. That door opened softly and a woman stepped

27

through, to pause there. Immediately thereafter Reno's set muscles loosened with astonishment. In this house, among this rough crew, was a beautiful woman.

She was no more than twenty-five. A mass of black hair sat loosely above a broad white forehead. Below that were slim, slightly olive features and eyes that were dark and alive and full of vital fire. She was straight, with the graceful sureness of a splendid body showing through the loose riding clothes she wore. And when she said: "What is it, Dad?" the throaty richness of the words sent long ripples across the room.

"Rae," said Big Lafe, "have you ever at any time seen this man before?"

Her glance turned on him and remained steady and solemn. Reno stiffened again and a blankness settled across his cheeks. He saw her lips part slightly. She seemed to bend forward while she studied him, to collect every item of his individuality in that long, long survey. Without any doubt, some quick reaction took place in her, for her hands half rose and fell. Then she turned her head swiftly toward Big Lafe. "No," she said in a kind of a breathless tone. "I never have."

"Never?" challenged The'dore's sullen voice.

"Never," said the girl.

"That's all," put in Big Lafe. "If you say you have never seen him, then he's a stranger. Your memory is longer than any I ever knew."

She started to turn back. Big Lafe cleared his throat and said slowly: "Two-Bits is dead, Rae."

The girl started, whirled about. Reno saw her eyes widen in pure pain, and then fill. But a moment later she was gone, closing the door behind her. Big Lafe spoke once more. "You'll stay here tonight, Reno. I'll show you a room. The'dore, see that his horse is put up."

"He belongs in the tool shed," muttered The'dore, "with a couple men guardin' him. You're foolish to trust—"

But Big Lafe swept that aside with an ironic calm. "I'll run the McMurtree affairs a few years longer yet,

The'dore. Reno, come with me." Taking up a nearby lamp, he slowly climbed the stairs and turned along the gallery. At one open door he halted, passed the lamp to the following Reno, and bowed with courteous gravity. "Trust you rest well," he said. "You are a smart man, Reno. You know more than appears on the record. And I do not doubt you have your own purposes to serve. For tonight we'll let the matter rest."

"What purpose," asked Reno with a show of idle curiosity, "would be bringing me to this country?"

"Don't know," answered Big Lafe. "But it'll soon be disclosed. No man can go it alone up here. Remember that. You're nobody's fool. Vilas picked you to do a chore—and he knows men. So do I. And you don't look like a hand to be running just for the fun of running."

"You're thinking maybe I'll be in your way?" suggested Reno.

"Remains to be seen," said Big Lafe, and looked more closely at Reno. "There is," he added with a heavy slowness, "a slight possibility you might be a help to me."

"When you've got it figured out," said Reno, "let me know."

"Good night."

Reno nodded and went in, closing the door. He placed the lamp on the small table by the bed, sat on the edge of that bed, and slowly removed his boots. Big Lafe's solid footsteps retreated down the stairway, and there was a rising hum of voices from below—broken by one angry accent that lifted and fell. In the adjoining room a board squealed slightly, bringing Reno's narrowed eyes against the flimsy partition. One boot in his hand, he got up, crossed to the only window, and from that point of view looked into the ranch yard. A man was at that moment leading his horse to the barn; and nearer at hand he saw a second fellow stolidly draped against the corral fence. The meaning of this one's location was clear enough. Pulling the shade down, Reno walked back to the bed.

"This much of it is accomplished," he said slowly

to himself. "It's a beginning—nothing more. The rest of it is going to be a lot harder."

His thoughts were broken by a soft drumming of finger tips against the wall. Once more riveting his attention there he saw what he had not noticed before—the four small seams of a doorway in that boarded surface, of a doorway without latch or keyhole or knob. Saying nothing—for the softness of the signal sounded to him more like a warning than an announcement—he sat quite still. Next moment the between-rooms door swung open and Rae McMurtree stood before him. One white hand rose with a gesture of caution and her eyes flashed toward the drawn shade.

"Why did you come here?" she demanded.

The Rifle Speaks Again

"To deliver a message to your dad."

She waved that aside with an impatient gesture of her small hand. "What else?"

"To deliver another one you probably didn't hear."

"What was it?"

"If it is to be told," answered Reno, "your dad will probably do the telling."

She had been crying. He could see that tears were not far off now. And the last words of the unfortunate Two-Bits occurred to him again. "There's only one woman to grieve for a black McMurtree." This, Reno suddenly realized, was the woman—and she was grieving. It prompted a gentler speech on his part.

"That young lad—that Two-Bits boy was thinking of you when he died."

"Stop it!" said Rae. "Do you want me to bring all the house up here?"

"Thought it was something you might want to know."

"I don't want to think of it now. I don't want to cry till I get out of here. Listen—why are you in these hills?"

"I've answered."

"No—you have not. Neither message brought you here. It is something else."

"How do you figure it?" demanded Reno.

The dark level eyes held his attention relentlessly. "You have fooled every man on the place. If you passed through Blackrock you probably fooled all the people there. But I know you. I remember you. When I stepped into the living room tonight I could have called your name."

31

"Why didn't you do it?" asked Reno.

For quite a while she didn't reply. But her head moved slowly from side to side, and the blackness of her eyes glowed with inner light. The lamp was behind her, and the glow of it softened the curves of her shoulders, broke into shining fragments along her hair. "Why are you here?" she asked more gently.

"I'm on the dodge. The sheriff is down in the valley. So I'm up in the hills. Is that plain enough, Rae?"

"Don't call me that!" she said sharply.

"Why not?"

The girl's answer was cool, frank. "Because you will betray me into calling you by your first name, in front of the crew."

"Old habits don't die easy," said Reno quietly. "I can remember a spotted horse with two stocking feet—"

"No!" protested the girl with a suppressed vehemence.

"All right," agreed Reno. "I'm not that man. He's dead. I came up here to deliver a message."

She stared at him for a long moment. Then she half whispered, "Jim, where are you going?"

"Away from this ranch in the morning, if I'm allowed."

"You will not be allowed."

Reno's glance sharpened a little. "Is that what you came to tell me?"

"Partly," said the girl. "Partly that and to warn you not to give yourself away to any man on this place. Never let anybody know what your real identity is or your real—purpose—whatever that may be. You are not with friends. There are McMurtrees in these hills who would betray you. I wanted to tell you that."

"Why?"

She reached out and took his hand and traced with her forefinger a slim white scar running across the heel of his palm. "I made that," she said very gently.

"So you're protecting me?"

She nodded. Yet her manner changed again, turned harder. "But listen to me. I am a McMurtree. All of me. And there is nothing in all this world I despise so much as those men who are set against us. All the

32

bitterness in my father's life, all his mistakes, all the violent things he has had to do are because of those men who hounded him, drove him here, made outlaws out of my kin."

"That's an explanation?"

"That," said the girl pointedly, "is a warning. I don't know yet what you are up to, or who you are working for. But should it be for those who are fighting us— I'll turn you over to the crew."

"Fair enough, Rae," said Reno, and was about to say something else when her quick signal of hand stopped him. On the instant she had turned and retreated to the other room, drawing the door behind her soundlessly. A body came up the stairs two at a time and rapidly down the gallery. Reno's door burst open and The'dore stood in the opening, his chest laboring with the quickness of his movement and his sullen eyes pinned to a Reno who stood calmly in his stocking feet and tapered off a cigarette. The'dore's mouth opened and closed. He walked across the room, brushing Reno back toward the bed, and rolled the shade up from the window angrily.

"You," he grunted, "leave that thing alone. Also, see that your light burns all night. Got it?"

"I understand English," drawled Reno.

"Let me have your gun," was The'dore's peremptory order. He stretched his rawboned fist outward. Reno, lighting his cigarette, studied the hand carelessly.

"No, I guess not."

"By God, you will!" breathed The'dore.

"Who's running this show, you or Big Lafe?" demanded Reno. "He said nothing about this gun. So I keep it. You want to call him up here and talk it over?"

The'dore swung about, walked to the doorway, and looked carefully along the gallery. When he came back it was to face Reno across a shoulder's distance—so close at hand that Reno saw the slate-green flecks in the man's odd, hostile eyes.

"All right," muttered The'dore. "If you understand English, try to get this clear. If McMurtree lets you ride

33

on tomorrow you see that you ride on—a damned long ways on. Don't light any campfires within thirty miles of this rancho. I don't want you around."

"You don't?" suggested Reno. "You personally don't?"

"That's right. *I* don't."

"And what worries you so much?" Reno wanted to know.

The'dore's stubborn jaws shot outward. "Nothing right now, mister. And I mean to see nothing does in the future. That's why I'm telling you. Sleep on it. You're old enough to know what happens when a little sound advice is disregarded." And with that last thrust, The'dore backed out of the room and shut the door. Reno stood on his feet long enough to hear the man cross the lower hall and leave it. Going to the window then he found the guard still posted by the corral, and presently saw The'dore come around the house corner and leave some terse order with the guard. The rest of the people of the ranch seemed to have settled for the night; no sound broke the pervading quiet inside this castle of the hills. Treading the narrow confines of his room, the last of the cigarette sputtering between his lips, Reno thought out his position with a studious intensity.

"One thing," he reflected, "appears plain. The old man runs affairs but he's got opposition on the part of this The'dore. That may mean something. Depends on how the rest of the crew throw their vote."

Afterwards he ground the stump of the cigarette between his fingers and rolled in for a welcome sleep.

Breakfast was a glum affair in a long mess hall back of the main room. Reno saw the strength of the McMurtree ranch for the first time and was mildly astonished at the number of hands present. There were, his quick count told him, more than twenty-five men on the place, and that meant another half-dozen out on remote chores. So the stiff and stern Big Lafe, who sat at the head of the table and drank a sparing cup of coffee, had thirty ready guns at his command. The'dore sat at the opposite end of the table, from which circumstance Reno judged

34

that the sullen one was more or less of a foreman. The'dore's cast of features was increasingly dour, and his eyes contained a sleepy surliness as if he had been up most of the night. The girl, at her father's immediate right, never glanced Reno's way during the meal.

After breakfast Reno strolled to the big hall. Then, nothing being said to him, he went on out into the crisp early sunshine that flooded over the treetops and streamed across the long meadow like running water. It was a high meadow, with the hint of sharply descending slopes beyond the timber. The air was thin and rich and Reno's cigarette had a fine savor to it. Yet as he idled toward the string of outbuildings he felt a portent of trouble coming from behind. None of the McMurtree people was to be seen—all of them had remained in the house. Hoisting himself to the top rail of a corral, he presently saw them leave the house, and from the scowling manner in which they broke across the yard, he knew they had been in a hot and heavy session. Big Lafe remained on the porch, his daughter with him. The'dore strode on to the barn, and in a little while Reno saw a group of men surrounding the foreman, all talking. Reno's ready mind leaped at the inevitable conclusion.

"Right there is the opposition. Big Lafe's hostile foreman has got ready followers."

His thoughts were broken by the old man's voice booming across the yard. "Get out a couple horses, The'dore! Don't stand there dreamin'!"

The'dore wrenched himself away from the group with an obstinate twist of his shoulders. The girl left the porch and came on toward Reno, slapping a romal carelessly against her breeches leg. A small felt hat sat insouciantly back on the dark head, and a beaded Indian jacket made a bright play of colors. But when she stopped in front of Reno he saw the sober cloud running across her eyes and the serious pursing of her lips.

"We're going for a little ride," she said.

Reno chuckled and slid down from the corral. "Who," he wanted to know, "is the escort and who is escorted?"

That broke her gravity. She smiled slightly back at him. "The gentleman usually escorts the lady. Suppose we let it go like that. I always make a tour in the morning."

The horses came up, led by a small-faced man who dropped the reins and stalked away. Rae McMurtree sprang to her saddle before Reno could get around to offer a hand and she was half across the meadow before he overtook her. In complete silence they rode to the tree line and went singlefile down a twisted trail that buckled at the bottom of a canyon and climbed the far side. It was a mile or better before they came to the heights of a ridge and were able to ride abreast.

"There's some purpose to this sashay?" queried Reno.

Rae looked at him fully, as if weighing that intent scrutiny on his features. Quite a while afterwards she said: "Are you always digging for purposes, Jim?"

"I have traveled pretty much alone," answered Reno with considerable thoughtfulness, "and have found little charity along the way. Somebody always wants something. It's been my policy to find out what. I have had to."

"And you've turned into a man that runs before a posse," she said rather bitterly. "What did you do? Was it very bad?"

"I am not a full-fledged outlaw," drawled Reno. "Let it go at that."

They were riding south along the ridge and from time to time past sweeping vistas of the far-off Blackrock plain. A few miles further, during which time not more than half a dozen words had been spoken, the girl swung with an apparent aimlessness to the west, and they came upon a lesser spur leading off toward that plain.

"My father," said the girl after a prolonged silence, "is a proud man. In some ways too proud. He looks backward—always backward. Somewhere in the Southern states there is a family plantation and a family record that lists the McMurtrees clear into Queen Elizabeth's time. One McMurtree was a captain in Drake's fleet.

One was a general in the Revolution. One was a senator. These are the things he remembers."

"And it's made him a little bitter?"

The girl's voice filled with energy. "Why shouldn't it? Until twenty years ago he was an honest man, a wealthy man, with a great ranch out there on that plain. He pioneered that country. Then the robbers came and the cattle war came and they fought him until he was bankrupt and they drove him up here with nothing to his name. They have been fighting him ever since. Well, what could he do but fight back? He has fought back. But the thing that hurts most is that he has had to fight as they fought—and that kind of fighting is without honesty. Do you see now?"

"Yes," said Reno, then thought of something else. "Who is this The'dore?"

She flashed him a swift, sharp glance. "You are quick to observe, aren't you? The'dore is our foreman. He came with us about two years ago. He is the only man—" and her voice sank a little as she said it— "who is not in some way related to me on the ranch."

She drew up then, for they had come to a point of land that fell sheerly into an off-running glen. A half mile beyond was a sweep of open meadow and over there sat a group of buildings gray in the brightness of the day—gray and disjointed. The girl pointed with a gloved hand and spoke again, more to herself than to him. "There's the sort of thing that happens in this country. Once upon a time, years ago, a family lived on that place. They were rich. They were respected. But when the cattle war came along they were between fires, too close to the hills, too close to the plains. The man tried to be neutral and consequently everybody hated him. So one night somebody ambushed Hi Benton and killed him. His wife and little boy had to move out. I used to play with that boy. I often wondered what happened to him."

Reno looked down at the place without visible expression. The silence lengthened out until it turned strained; and the girl at last said: "If I have brought back unpleasant memories, Jim, I'm sorry."

Reno looked at her. "That's all right, Rae." He went on thoughtfully, "I was surprised last night when you recognized me as Hi Benton's son. I didn't think you'd remember me. It's been a great many years. Everything's changed. I haven't got the same body, and same face, or the same mind. Not another soul in this country recognized me. How was it that you did?"

"Never mind," murmured the girl. "Perhaps it is because I always expected you to come back. Perhaps there were things I never forgot—about you. But the moment I stepped into the room and saw you I knew. As it was, I almost betrayed you—almost called your right name."

"Wait a minute. We've got to get this straight. I was Jim Benton until three months ago. When I decided to come here, I changed my name. I had to do that; I had to get a new name and a new frame of mind so that nobody would ever come up behind me, call out my old name and take me off guard. I went to another part of the country as Jim Reno. I practiced on that name until it was more mine than the old one. Then I lit out for here."

"And you changed your habits, too?" asked the girl, a little forlornly. "To the extent that you came here with a posse on your heels? I'm sorry."

"Don't be too sorry," he warned her. "But I had to make certain changes. This is a dangerous game I'm playing."

"What game?" asked the girl.

Reno watched her, wondering at the discouragement visible on her clear cheeks. "You ought to know what would bring me back. When Dad was killed, Mother and I had to leave. What could a woman and a small kid do? We went to another valley—and I had to grow up and become the man of the family. That hurt, Rae. It's been hurting ever since. All these years I've had the killing of my dad on my mind. Never forgot it, never let it die. Mother had a pretty rough time. But she always paid taxes on this old place, just to keep it. We never knew who used it or lived in it. Still, we kept it. When I got old enough, she made me promise not to come here. She was afraid. I kept the promise. Right up till she died, which was about six months ago. Then I made my plans." His voice chilled and he spoke more slowly. "I'm back now to find out who killed Dad. That's the whole story."

"Your mother was right," breathed the girl. "You shouldn't be here. You will never be able to uncover that mystery. But if you do, you will be killed."

He shook his head. "That's why I'm here. I don't think I'll ever leave this land again. Now remember, Rae. My name is Jim Reno. Even when you think of me, think of me as Reno, so that your tongue won't slip. I have put the old name behind me. Forgotten it. It's dead—and will be until I have learned all that I want to learn."

"All right," said Rae McMurtree quietly.

Reno turned toward the little valley below, pointing. "Who uses the ranch now?"

"It's free range," said the girl. "Though there's always cattle grazing on it—and usually some party or another using it for occasional shelter."

"Rae, what's the gossip around here—about my dad's death?"

"Only whispers," mused the girl. "You've got to realize that nobody cared much about you people. The McMurtrees didn't trust your father because he didn't have anything to do with them. The Vilas faction, as I get it, was always more or less afraid of him. That's all I know. But I've been sorry, so very sorry."

"Plenty in this country to feel sad about," said Reno briefly, and reined his horse around.

They started back along the same trail, wandered off into another glen. Once they saw the distant housetops of a settlement which Reno guessed to be Morgantown. Afterwards the thick forest enveloped them, and it was past high noon when they cantered into the Mc-Murtree clearing. Reno got down.

"What was the purpose of this ride?" he demanded bluntly.

The girl studied him at length and seemed to make up her mind. "For one thing, to see if you'd try to break away. I'm glad you didn't."

Reno turned half about and nodded his head at the timber. The'dore was just then emerging from the trees. "I knew better than to try," said Reno. "He was within gunshot all the way—waiting for me to break."

The girl revealed a quick disappointment. "Was that all that kept you from running?"

"No. I wouldn't have tried in any event. I'm here to weather it through, Rae."

"I'm glad to hear you say so," said the girl. "As for the rest of my purpose, it was to find why you came here. I was told to get the reason from you if I could."

"And now," said Reno grimly, "you can go back to your dad and report."

"When you want to be," observed the girl sadly, "you are very, very hard. I am not telling my father why you are here. Or who you are."

"Why not?"

"Before that happens, I want you to find out something for yourself."

"Which is what?"

"I want you to find out," said the girl more energetically, "whether or not a McMurtree fired the shot that got your father." Then she bent nearer—for The'dore was slowly closing up—and whispered: "If you have any eyes at all you can see that my father is in trouble and that this ranch is badly split. Perhaps—perhaps, Jim you may be able to help. Nobody else can or will. I have little hope."

The'dore rode abreast and spoke heavily. "Had your parade, I see."

The girl turned without answering and walked to the house. Reno, feeling hungry, followed at a more indolent pace. At the door he paused to look around. The'dore's sultry, Mongol eyes were unwinkingly set on him.

The afternoon turned hotter. All across the cloudless sky the sun's wide bands flashed and burned; and for the space of two hours or more the men of the Mc-Murtree ranch vanished into the shade of the scattered quarters. Left completely to himself, Reno sat awhile on the main house porch until his muscles cramped on him and a sense of restlessness drove him over to the yard as far as the barn. Crouched there in the semitwilight of that structure's long stable-way, he drew aimless patterns in the dust while his cool mind went ferreting amongst the possibilities. Like all solitary travelers, he relied a great deal on his instincts and those sudden waves of premonition that came out of so much thin air to prompt him and to place him on guard. And now he felt quite clearly that the drowsing lull about him was aripple with crosscurrents of trickery and deceit. There was something in the offing, some sure face-about of events. Thus when around four o'clock The'dore came from one of the bunkhouses and went to the main house at a rapid stride, Reno felt half relief and half excitement.

The'dore walked in with the swaggering sureness of one whose power was certain enough to depend on. Reno even heard the man calling Big Lafe's name throughout the great hall, calling it peremptorily. After that, quiet returned, but the McMurtree crew began to appear in the yard, two at a time. One of these ostentatiously walked to the barn and halted there. Half a dozen strolled indolently toward the main house porch and took station there. The rest of the outfit straggled from point to point, revealing a fretful uncertainty.

All this, however, was changed when The'dore again made his appearance on the porch. His voice lifted through the quiet afternoon like the echo of a brazen horn. "Billy, you stay at the stable. Everybody else come in here." In response, all the men went to the house with an ill-concealed alacrity, except the man nearest Reno. He came closer and leaned against the barn wall.

41

"It'll be all right, I suppose," drawled Reno ironically, "if I scratch my nose?"

The man only glowered and continued his bald-faced watchfulness. Reno shifted position, retracing the patterns he had drawn in the dust. There were definite rumors of high and angry talk from the main house. Sharp echoes rolled across the yard. A hand started to walk through the door, was arrested by a curt order, and turned in again with a morose shake of his head. Time passed slowly, and even the guard began to fiddle in his tracks. Looking at his watch, Reno was surprised to find it was after five. A short while after that the meeting broke up and the crew appeared.

The'dore strode toward the corrals with part of the outfit compactly around him, and Reno, studying all this with a deep watchfulness, suddenly thought that this group adhering to the foreman was larger than the one he had observed in the morning. If it meant anything, he reflected, it meant that The'dore had won so many more converts to his particular scheme—whatever that was. The rest of the bunch followed to the corrals more slowly. Some of them broke away and headed in the direction of the bunkhouses. When these fellows came into view again they were armed.

Meanwhile heavy dust rolled out of the corrals. Fresh ponies were led into the yard, saddled and left standing by the main house porch. All this went on with a show of hurried energy. The'dore spoke a subdued word to a pair of men near him and those, immediately mounting, went away to the south just as the supper triangle began to beat up the brassy eddies of sound. Without further invitation, Reno went in to eat. When he returned again to the porch the sun had fallen and the long folds of dusk were sweeping down the sky. Big Lafe came through the door and stood beside him.

"You'll ride with the men tonight," he said abruptly.

"Where to and what for?" asked Reno.

"The question will answer itself in due course," observed Big Lafe. Then he added, "You are entitled to a reason, of course. It is very simple. The men feel that if you are a party to possible trouble this evening you'll be in the middle of it with them."

"Sound politics," applauded Reno dryly. "I take it I am not free to leave this ranch and less welcome to stay."

"Your coming here has brought a complication I never expected," said Big Lafe. "I will not explain the remark. But unless you are a dumber man than I rig you to be, you'll be able to amplify the thought."

"A fellow learns a lot just driftin' with the tide, or lazin' around the barn door."

"I thought you would."

"McMurtree," said Reno, unexpectedly frank, "take this for what it's worth. But if you expect to deal the same brand of cards you been dealin' for a number of years you better get another jack of spades. The card is worn out, full of thumb marks."

McMurtree turned and started to speak, but was prevented by the appearance of the outfit filing across the yard. The'dore's face was blurred in the gathering dusk as he let his harsh words fall. "All right, Reno. Here's your rig."

"The'dore," said Big Lafe, "I'll be going with you. Get my pony."

The'dore sat back in the saddle and grunted his surprise. "It will be the first time in a coon's age. What for?"

"When I get to the point of explainin' my mind to you," said Big Lafe, "it will be a sorry world. Get my pony."

"There's no need of it," argued The'dore. "I'm able to take care of this. If you want it plain, I'd like you to stay here. We travel fast."

"Damn you—get my pony!" boomed Big Lafe. "When I speak I intend to be obeyed!"

The'dore let out a great gust of breath, but said nothing. A ranch hand on the flanks of the party silently wheeled away to the barn, the hoofs of his horse breaking crisply into the falling night. A wind ran gently across the porch and Reno, all at once full of admiration for this old bitten wolf of the hills, saw Big Lafe's hair ruff up grizzled on his head. Then man stood there like a rock, implacable and without the knowledge of fear or physical weakness. And he spoke again to his foreman with a cutting calm. "You are growing too big for your pants, The'dore. On my pay sheet you're listed as a common hand. Don't forget that and don't make it necessary for me to remind you of it again."

"The day is about gone," said The'dore with rage guttering in his throat, "when you can speak to me like that! Here and now I warn you against tryin' it again!"

All the rest of the outfit seemed to have quit breathing. Rae came out of the hall, coming between her father and Reno. The hand came back with the old man's horse and held the reins out. The'dore said almost under his breath, "All right," and spurred out of the group. Big Lafe walked slowly to his saddle and climbed up. Reno, on the verge of following, heard the girl's bated whisper:

"Don't let The'dore ride beside you alone."

Reno left the porch and stepped to the leather. At that the group wheeled away, two and two, and cantered across the meadow. Short of the little trail through the timber the leaders, The'dore and Big Lafe, wheeled downgrade and left the clearing behind. Far below in a tangle of brush and rocks, Reno looked around to see the house lights shining out into a world finally gone dark. There was no talk amongst the men and no sense of lightness. Half a mile up the canyon, the file tackled a stiff hill, crawled to the summit of a ridge, and stretched out to a steady run. The country opened up for a considerable distance, and once Reno got the glimmer of Morgantown in a distant hollow. When that reflection died behind the trees there was only the thin cold glitter of the stars above. Two miles of this steady pacing ended without warning in a complete halt. A sibilant murmur ran the line and certain men detached themselves from it and trotted ahead. Cow smell came up the wind. Then the cavalcade pointed into another of the countless depressions, and within the

44

space of minutes they were on the sides of a compact group of cattle.

The herd had been previously bunched and made ready. That much was plain to Reno. What also was plain to him was that Big Lafe's outfit had done this enough times before to have perfected a discipline that needed no added ordering. The group shifted left and right until there was only a single man at Reno's side—and this one obviously instructed to remain so. A lantern suddenly flashed and went out after describing a complete circle. At that signal cattle and men moved forward, downgrade. Somewhere ahead The'dore called out, "Billy," and the man beside Reno answered, "'T's all right." Another rider cut back and came up on Reno's other flank.

"I've got this taken care of," announced Billy with a trace of belligerence.

"What are you trying to do?" said Big Lafe's stiff voice. "Notify the county we're abroad? Get the hell up forward and tell The'dore to keep his mouth shut."

"All right," grumbled Billy. "Didn't know it was you." And afterwards he pulled away and vanished among the sidling shadows.

The clearing fell into a long decline well sloped to either side—an admirable runway for night driving. All this had the earmarks of thoughtful planning. By the feel of the mass moving ahead, Reno judged there were no more than a hundred beefs in the bunch, which was a two- or three-man job instead of a job needing the present twenty-odd hands. So the extra hands, he concluded, were meant for trouble—the trouble that comes of moving stolen cattle at night. This was an old story, and he pieced out the rest of it with no great strain of thinking. It fell into a pattern. The stock had been gathered a few head at a time, thrown into the secretive pocket, and held there till the herd was made. What went on now was a drive to some receiver elsewhere in the hills who would push the beef on to market. Big Lafe McMurtree, the descendant of captains and statesmen, had turned to this.

45

It was a sorry fact to be hitched to the spartan, admirable old man beside him. And thinking of it, Reno spoke his mind aloud.

"You're letting me into the whole story, McMurtree."

It was a long time before Big Lafe answered. "There was a date in history," he finally muttered, "when a brigand was considered a good citizen. Writers wrote stories about them. I don't hold any such illusions. A cattle thief is a cattle thief, which is what I am. But what lies behind all this is something you don't know. You see damned little of the story here. Let it ride like that—for a while. The rest will come soon enough."

A rider pushed his way back beside the old man and murmured something indistinct. Big Lafe answered with a brief explanation. "Turn short at Sweetgrass Creek and go across the bridge." The rider went forward again, and presently the momentum of the herd was temporarily checked. The flank men began to crowd against the cattle, romals slapping down. Confusion rose from the front and a trenchant cursing. But it lasted only a little while and Reno, coming along the dusty rear, felt the ground shift upward as the trail bent. He splashed across a narrow ford, passed into timber. A little later he arrived at the top of a ridge and found the trail wheeling again—once more pitching downward. The wind freshened. At the end of three tedious miles, Reno found the unbroken expanse of the prairie lying below and beyond. He knew then where he was, for in the distance—in the far western distance—the lights of Blackrock winked through the gloom.

"These cattle," he thought, "were probably rustled from that prairie. Now they're going back to the prairie. Which is damned odd."

Hardly had he come to the conclusion when a signal flash appeared off to the immediate left—a lantern uncloaked and held high. In another moment it was concealed again, but the circling McMurtree hands had seen the warning and instantly began circling the herd to check it. The light appeared again, more briefly; a rider posted back from the head of the column and reined in beside Big Lafe. The'dore's voice said: "Well, sir?"

"Come along," answered Big Lafe.

The two of them turned abreast and aimed for that point where the light had been. A cow began to bellow dismally in the shifting, spreading bunch. Reno, mind racing down the channels of his own scheming, wheeled and retreated a good fifty yards. Here he halted.

"There's the receiver of the stolen goods," he thought. "Him with the light. But what the hell? What's the point in running the beef back to where it came from?"

The forms of Big Lafe and The'dore merged with the yonder shadows. Once the light rose straight from the earth, and Reno dimly viewed the form of that third party, the receiver. Then the light went out. There was a parley going on, a very short parley terminated by Big Lafe's voice calling calmly back, "All right, boys." And at the order the hands began to drift toward Reno. The job was done, the transfer made. On the sharp lookout, Reno saw Big Lafe and The'dore appear in the night.

"If I want to get clear of this outfit," Reno warned himself, "here is the best chance I'll ever have. If I stay on I'll have The'dore to handle before another day's done."

Something strange crossed the night like a rolling cloud of fog. All the McMurtree hands had gathered a few yards away and were sitting in their saddles—all queerly still and speechless. Big Lafe and The'dore advanced at a trot, but within the length of ten yards one of them—Reno thought it was The'dore—swerved aside and went on at a slightly faster pace. A slow, cautious call rose from the McMurtree ranks.

"Lafe—where's the rest of these fellows?"

"It is none of our business where they are," answered Lafe, now turning beside Reno. "Our job is done—come on."

The'dore's lunging yell came from behind the cattle furiously: "Watch out—watch out!"

And then the night exploded. A concerted stuttering

47

roar of gunfire smashed the calm of the hillside and the echoes bounded off the earth enormously. Stripes of purple crimson painted the darkness a hundred yards off to the eastward—over in the direction the receiver had been; dust rose around Reno, dust kicked up by the thudding lead. A McMurtree hand cried out as if his heart were breaking, and the ponies began pitching in a senseless, jammed-up confusion. A form raced at Reno, cursed his blackest rage, and went screaming to the ground. The herd broke like water through a caving dam—thundering off toward the valley. Somewhere, farther away than before, The'dore yelled again, the meaning of his words quite lost.

Reno crouched low in the leather, watching that long row of flame points glow and die and glow. And in that fraction of time he knew there was only one answer—a quick retreat. He curbed his pitching horse and pushed beside Big Lafe, who seemed to have been stricken on the spot.

"Here, get out of this! Call your boys out of it!"

Big Lafe had no answer. The old man was sitting stiff in the saddle and he was facing the fire. Reno reached over to catch the reins of the other's pony and missed. He had no more chance, for the McMurtree hands broke and came racing on. The weight of that flight carried Reno away from Big Lafe. His horse was hit dead on, went to its knees, and got up again. Some of the Mc-Murtree crew began to answer the shots, aiming with an unthinking recklessness; and the blast of one of those guns stung Reno's neck. Meanwhile the opposing fusilade was veering, coming closer. Slugs struck all around him. Another McMurtree rider fell, shouting up from beneath the mad, churning hoofs. Reno was hit again by a passing hand and then, knowing he had lost all contact with Big Lafe, he hauled his horse around and fought through the press of brute and man. He literally plowed a trail into the clear—to find himself eventually on the margin of some stunted pines and quite alone.

The firing fell short of him. The McMurtree outfit had left the open. Over to his left front he heard the brush being smashed down and men calling from point to point. Immediately after that the gun reports began to thicken and crash faster into the sky. At the same time he detected a definite shift in the fighting. The play of sound from the ambushers subsided considerably, and while he sat there in the saddle, detached and coolly considering, he made out a turning movement of those ambushers. They stopped the barrage of lead completely for as long a space as it took to draw half a dozen deep breaths. Then suddenly—for everything happened with a whiplike speed—a long and strung-out shadow undulated across the far edge of the open area and vanished down the grade. At that the McMurtrees began to halloo like hounds on the scent. They gathered in the brush, came out of it, and flung themselves by the immovable Reno; and presently they too were lost off there on the heels of the ambushers. The echo of an occasional shot rose to mark their running.

"They'll be scattered all over the hills from now till daylight," he said. "And a lot of blood will be left in the sand." Then, poised with all his senses searching the night, he was aware of a stir on the lower reaches of the clearing. Instinctively, Reno bent forward and placed a hand over the nostrils of his pony, seeing a shadow drift up and halt. All he made out was a tall form on a horse, and even that was presently blurred as the man circled the clearing once and then went off at a drumming speed.

Reno gathered up the reins and started off. "I have got to go back to the ranch," he decided grimly, "and come to a showdown with those boys. If I run now they'll hunt me all through the hills and I'll get nothing done." Then an entirely different thought displaced the lesser items in his mind, and he dwelt on it with a studied interest and an increasing suspicion. "The'dore got behind the protection of the cattle before the firing started. When he shouted he was away off from the trouble. When he shouted the second time he was still further off. Now I wonder if it was The'dore who crossed the clearing just now?"

He carried that wonder all the way to a high point of the hills and then dismissed it in the face of a more immediately important consideration, which was to find the way back to the ranch. One ridge and another fooled him, a half dozen trails led him into the blindness of untraveled canyons. And when at last he picked up the clear light of the McMurtree house, the sky overhead was paling and day hovered just below the eastern rim. At the edge of the meadow he reined in, mistrusting his own choice of tactics, but after a moment he pushed on to the porch. There was no sign of life in the yard and no evidence of returned hands. But when he opened the door and strode inside he saw Big Lafe standing by a dying fire with the girl beside him.

Big Lafe made no gesture, but he said harshly: "So you came back."

— 4 —

Crossplay

"What else was there to do?" asked Reno, crossing the room.

"You might have kept going," muttered Big Lafe.

A sudden break of light appeared on the girl's solemn cheeks. There was an actual blaze of feeling in her eyes as she turned to the old man. "I knew he would!" she cried. "I told you he would! He had no part in that trap!"

"No," said Reno. "I didn't."

"You might have kept going," repeated Big Lafe.

"Sure. And that would have clinched me with your boys. I couldn't stay in the hills that way. They'd hunt me all over hell's half acre."

"You consider they'll believe you for a minute?" asked Big Lafe. And he answered his own question with a shake of his head. "No. You're done for on this range."

"You're giving me my walkin' papers?"

"For your own good."

Reno reached for his cigarette tobacco and shook out a smoke, scowling over the job. When he looked up there was an added sharpness of expression on his face. "It fits better into my plans to stay here and tough it through."

"I knew you had your own irons in the fire," muttered Big Lafe. "That stuck out all over you."

Reno looked to the girl, but she shook her head slightly. Then he added: "Men ain't back? No, I didn't suppose they would be. They'll be scattered forty miles all ways and drag in one at a time. I don't get this ambush stuff but it'll come to me sooner or later. Seems to be more crooked turns to the road than I figured." He lighted a match and touched it to the cigarette tip. His eyes were bright and hard. "McMurtree, your foreman is a scoundrelly dog."

"I know that," said Big Lafe.

"So?" grunted Reno. "You already knew it? And you keep him on?"

Big Lafe nodded and Reno, watching the old man's face, said reflectively: "So it's like that? You've got him and you can't get shut of him. He's too much to fire."

Big Lafe made no answer, yet Reno saw agreement written on that bold, tired face. It moved him to say something he had not meant to say. "You can take this for what you think it's worth, but The'dore was pretty well out of range when the trouble started. Away behind the cattle. I doubt if he ever came into the play. And somebody came back from the brush after it was all over—somebody that might have been friend The'dore. I think he's using you, McMurtree."

The girl raised her head. "I have never trusted him."

Big Lafe showed an increasing weariness. Abruptly he turned to his daughter. "Rae, you know something about this man here that I don't know. That's true?"

"Yes."

"What is it?"

She pointed one slim finger at Reno, who said briefly: "Let it ride a little longer. I have business here."

Big Lafe spoke to the girl again, more insistently. "You trust him?"

"Yes," said Rae. "Completely."

Big Lafe squared his shoulders and let out a deep breath. "Reno," said he, "I know you're not a crook. I also know you've got a level head. What I don't know is how good a fighter you are. But that's your risk, not mine. How about it?"

"What do you want done?" was Reno's prompt answer.

"I want you to go tell Vilas to draw off quick. If he don't there'll be another war. I can't stop my boys, and

I don't want to see them killed. Vilas has got to draw out."

The girl showed puzzlement. "Vilas?" she said. "What has he to do with us? He's no friend of ours."

"It is something even you don't know," said Big Lafe wearily. "Reno, you've caught on?"

"I sort of suspected the message Vilas sent you was misleadin'," drawled Reno.

"It was not a threat," agreed Big Lafe. "It was an arrangement. The key of it was his reference to the base of Drum Rock. That is where we went tonight with the cattle."

"I don't understand," said the girl.

"It had better be explained now," was Big Lafe's answer. "You've always known we rustled stock off the prairie, Rae."

"Yes," said the girl in a low voice. "I have. It's been something that hurt me to know, Dad. But I have tried to excuse you because of the things those people on the plain have done to you."

"There is no excuse for thievin'," muttered Big Lafe. "I make none for myself. In the beginning I did it out of bitterness. After I got started it was something hard to stop. The boys were set on getting their revenge. I figured it better to let them have this revenge that way than to go out and start another killin' contest. But it has been in my mind to make an end to it a long while. I would have done so, except that The'dore came along. My counsel of moderation was no good against The'dore. He could always stir the boys to a crazy pitch. So now he thinks he's bigger than I am. I begin to believe he is."

"He is," said Reno bluntly.

"But what about Vilas?" asked the girl.

"Years ago Vilas was the leader against me in the war. Since I have come to the hills, he's continued this leadership—apparently. But some few years back he came secretly to me and said we might both profit. The man's a crook and a sly one. He suggested I enlarge the rustlin' business. Steal from everybody on the plain, includin' himself. Then he'd arrange to take the rustled stuff at

53

fit occasions and market it. It was an easy way for me to make money. Nobody ever suspected Vilas, of course, because he had helped drive me out of the plain. He had only one man in on the secret—which was this foreman of his, Hale Wolfert. Wolfert handles everything. Wolfert's got his own separate crew who consider it a deal that Wolfert is puttin' over on Vilas and everybody else. Nobody on our side knows of it—except The'dore. All the rest of the boys are in the dark. All they know is that somebody comes up after night, meets me, and gets the beef. They've never even seen Wolfert's face."

The girl slowly turned away, walked to the far side of the fireplace. Big Lafe watched her out of his fine, troubled eyes, and he said gently: "It is just another piece of the general scheme of thievin', Rae. I make no excuses. I will say I have tried to stop. But The'dore holds the whip over the boys now. Not me."

"Then get rid of him!" said the girl with a sudden strength.

"I am older than I thought I was," Big Lafe answered; and in that answer Reno heard a profound sadness, a heavy burden of regret. He threw his cigarette into the fire.

"All right, I'll go tell Vilas."

"And then what?" demanded the girl. "We're no better off. The'dore is still here. What will we do?"

"I'll come back," said Reno, the words dropping softly into the stillness of that great room. "And maybe we can figure it out."

"You'll never be safe on this ranch," warned Big Lafe.

"I have known very little safety in the last few years," reflected Reno, looking into the fire. "And mighty little sense of comfort. What's the odds? I came here to do a chore. This business fits in. That's all, the whole story of it. So long till I see you again."

He went across the room and out the door to his horse. But he had not yet turned away when he heard the girl calling to him. She came over the porch and stood at the beast's side, looking up with her oval features dimly outlined in the coming gray dawn. Her hand rose and touched him.

"Jim," she whispered, "you are riding among hard men. The hardest men in the world. Whatever you've done that was wrong, I don't care. But you've got to watch out for yourself. If you go out, what is there left—for me?"

"Old times are hard to forget," murmured Reno. "I'll be back." And he rode off across the meadow, down the little trail. At the end of two miles he came to the Morgantown-Blackrock road just as the sunless morning broke about him and the mist wreathes began to evaporate. He went rapidly, sharply attuned to the promise of the unexpected. And when he arrived at a side trail some distance beyond the main height of the range, he swung into it for safety's sake and pushed on for another mile or so. At this point he deserted the trail altogether and swung in Blackrock's direction again, pushing through the heavy brush and sapling stands. He followed the spine of a little ridge to its tip, angled into a rough canyon bottom; and about sunup he turned a bend and came upon a glade encircled by heavy virgin timber. As he did so all the weight of shock drove his rein arm into a checking gesture. Ahead—only a hundred feet ahead—Hale Wolfert crouched over a wisp of fire. The sound of Reno's approach was small enough, yet it stiffened the man instantly. He shot to his full ungainly height and whirled about, reaching for the blackened gunbutt at his side. Reno, coldly realizing there was no other course open, swayed in the saddle and made a swift grab for his own weapon. But as his fingers closed about it he heard a vindictive voice come from behind him.

"You're covered. Stop the draw."

It took Reno off his guard, it completed his rout. All he could do was check his try. Completely covered—for Wolfert's gun had risen to a steady aim, he understood now that his only chance of survival rested on the deliberateness of his surrender. That moment became an hour and the silence went flat and breathless. Mastering the savage impulse to make a fight of it, he slowly dragged his hand from the gun and turned still more slowly in the saddle to face the rear man.

It was The'dore. The'dore's eyes were red slashes and his mouth a pale crease. "Put up your hands," said The'dore. "Put 'em up as high as you ever reached."

Reno started to obey. Then the turning morning broke apart and a long echo swelled up the canyon. Wolfert had fired. Reno felt something strike the side of his head with all the stunning effect of a club. The world faded and he fell without a murmur, the strength fainting out of him. As from an enormous distance he heard the gun roar again. After that he knew nothing.

5

The War Plot

When he came out of the deep stupor a dull ache knocked against his head in rhythm with his pulse and the bitter taste of blood was in his mouth. All the side of his face was wet, his battered nerves were trembling along shoulder and neck. He felt weak, very weak, and so for a while he made no attempt to move or to open his eyes. That—the sense of being detached from himself—was what saved him. For the pervading silence into which he wakened was a moment later broken by a voice, and that voice acted on him in the manner of water thrown over his face. It screwed his faculties up and even checked the throbbing of his brain. Motionless, eyes closed, he identified those churlish and bitten-off tones as belonging to The'dore.

"—can't stay here forever, Wolfert. Won't do if some of the McMurtree boys stumble into us. They're all over the hills."

"We've got to talk this out."

"Talk it quick then. Your shots made a hell of a racket—and didn't do much good either. Reno's only creased. He'll pull himself together pretty soon. Then what're we going to do with him?"

"If he hadn't swung around when I fired I'd got him right in the gizzard."

"Which has nothing to do with the facts. What'll we do with him? He's on to us. We can't let him pack that secret around."

"Maybe the next slug will land better," said Wolfert slowly, suggestively.

Reno heard these words trail into the dreaming stillness of the morning. The men were behind him. Knowing this, he opened his eyes a little and saw his horse standing twenty yards off, cropping the grass. The'dore spoke with a rough hastiness.

"You do it then."

"Leave it to me," said Wolfert.

"Damn, but you're a cool sport!"

"What's the difference?" droned Wolfert. "But we've got to talk this out. Our little play last night worked all right, didn't it?"

"I blamed near didn't get out of range before your men opened up. You might've waited another count of ten after I shouted."

"The boys was a little quick," admitted Wolfert. "I hadn't no more than stopped back from meetin' you and Big Lafe before they started shootin'. The trouble was, your bunch started away from the clearin' quick and they'd been beyond hittin' in another second. If you want my opinion, Big Lafe acted cagey. It was the first time he ever cut the meetin' so short."

"I think," said The'dore slowly, "that the bunch smelled something. I think they felt something in the breeze."

"Well, it will turn out just like we wanted it to turn out. The McMurtrees will figure they were led into a double cross. They'll go hog wild. They'll start the war up again."

"No," contradicted The'dore. "They'll think some other rustlin' outfit timed it to cut in. They don't know who's behind the play. Big Lafe is the only one that knows about Vilas."

"That's where you come in," said Wolfert. "When you go back to the ranch you spill that. Say Vilas is in it. Say he arranged this affair. That'll make 'em ready to come down off the hills."

"Yeah? How would I know this? They'll ask me where I got my information."

"Easy," explained Wolfert. "You tell the McMurtrees you saw me and a couple other Vilas hands rushin' through the timber about daylight."

"That puts you in no comfortable position."

"I'll keep out of the way," answered Wolfert dryly. "I can afford to take the chance in a game like this."

But The'dore was finding flaws. "Vilas," he said, "will drop you when he finds out you put on this show. It means the end of his arrangement with Big Lafe."

"Who's to tell him I put on the show?" demanded Wolfert. "I'll explain to him some other outfit cut in on us. No, I'll do better. I'll tell him some of your outfit double-crossed us. That'll finish the Vilas-McMurtree agreement right there."

"How about your own particular crew of bunch jumpers?"

"They never did know Vilas was in this rustling. All they know is that I'm running an independent game. It's to their benefit. They won't talk. They can't afford to." Then Wolfert's voice went dryer than before. "They know what would happen if they did talk. I have spent a lot of time pickin' those jugheads. I know what they can do and what they won't do. There ain't a hand in the bunch that dares pull out—he'd never get clear."

"So you're fixed to go through with this?"

"*We're* fixed to go through with it," amended Wolfert.

Reno suffered a tremendous desire to move his cramped arms. The sun burnt against his skin and the dust bit at it; his throat stuck and he had to throw all his will against the impulse to cough. His gun had been taken—that much he knew from the lack of weight on his right hip. Yet occupied as he was by the physical torment, he followed each man's talk with a puzzled attention. It was clear enough that they were in partnership for some design of their own. What he could not arrive at was the nature of the design. The'dore was talking again with a reluctance that at once stamped him as the weaker of the two. It was he who held back and offered objections while Wolfert relentlessly argued them aside.

"There's two men you'll never fool," said The'dore. "This Reno—"

"I'll take care of him," cut in Wolfert.

"—and Big Lafe," added The'dore. "Big Lafe is too smart not to guess what it's all about."

"Then you take care of him."

"Not so fast," protested The'dore. "I can swing the outfit against him. I can take authority away from him. Any time I want. They'll listen to me when I say, 'Let's go wipe out the desert.' I can do that. But I can't frame Big Lafe and draw on him. You've got to remember all those boys have got a little of Big Lafe's blood in them. They wouldn't stand for it a minute."

"Then," said Wolfert with a grunt of finality, "I'll take care of him, too."

"How?"

"Leave that to me. But we're ready to go on to the next stage of the game. You go back to the ranch. Talk the outfit up to the killin' point. Tomorrow night go down and raid Blackrock. Rip it to pieces and draw back home again. That shouldn't be so hard. Tomorrow's Tuesday and there'll be few punchers in the town. But the attack will put every prairie rancher on the warpath. They'll organize and bring a party up to attack McMurtree. Then the ball is open, my lad. Anything is high, wide, and handsome. And while all this is going on there'll be damned few hands watching the stock on the range. I'll have my boys comb it clean. Ain't that simple enough? The McMurtrees will get the blame for doing it. You and I will clean up a young fortune."

"While the scrap lasts," grumbled The'dore.

"It will last a long time. The last war went on for two years. That's where Vilas made his money. Nibbled off the cattle from the ranches which were too busy fightin' to watch their own interests."

At that instant Reno had the whole thing explained, and he wondered at his own failure not to have comprehended it before. During a range war all bars were down. Anything could happen—as Hale Wolfert meant should happen now. But again The'dore was arguing.

"I'm to lead these fellows into Blackrock?"

"You've got to take a chance once in a while," pointed out Wolfert impatiently. "What ails you? All you do is keep the McMurtrees scrapping and running. I do the rest. You get your profits out of me. That ain't the whole story either. When this thing is finished we may have the prairie outfits ready to make a dicker for peace. Thirty men, you want to realize, can run a whole county ragged. Well, if it works out that way you'll be the kingpin in the hills. It's your country altogether. Big Lafe will be dead or he'll have no more authority over his men. Point is, keep these lads whipped up. They're a hard bunch and they like to fight."

The'dore said, "We've done enough palaverin'."

"It's settled then. Tomorrow night you ride."

"Yeah," agreed The'dore with no great amount of enthusiasm. "But we've got to do something about this Reno."

Reno went cold. He heard the two approach, boots scuffing the soft dirt. One of them walked around. The other stood in back. Through a fractional slit of his lids he saw one pair of long legs within reach of his arms, and he knew then what he would do. It was a thin chance, but all that he had.

"Get it over with," said The'dore nervously. "Me, I don't care for cold turkey."

There was a long pause. Wolfert, behind, wasn't moving, and there was no sound of an arm reaching for a gun. Reno's nerves were like filaments of ice, and he cocked his mind for the outward lunge that was to bring The'dore down by the heels. Then he heard Wolfert saying reflectively: "No-o, I got a better idea. I'll take him along. He may be a help to me."

Reno, relaxing, was not prepared for what followed. Wolfert let out a grunt and struck with his boot, catching Reno in the small of the back. "You!" snapped Wolfert. "Come out of it!"

Reno's head rolled and he dug the nails of his fingers deep into his palms to hold himself from springing up. He opened his eyes, staring directly into Wolfert's lowered face.

"Get up!" said the Vilas foreman.

Reno pulled himself to his knees, staggered to his feet. A gray screen fell across the day and he thought he was falling. Wolfert seized him and shook him about with a vindictive pleasure. "Come out of it—you're lucky to be here! I've had two chances at you and passed up both. If you ever get out of this, Reno, you'll maybe learn a little something about deliverin' messages."

The'dore swung around and walked off to his horse. "Too much talk, Wolfert," he said over his shoulder, and then climbed to the saddle. A moment later he disappeared around the bend. A pair of jays began screaming at the top of a pine, and Reno felt his head clear up. Wolfert's cavilling features were distinctly before him.

"Get aboard," said the Vilas foreman and turned carelessly away. But a dozen paces onward he whipped his lank body around, of a sudden wolfishly enraged. "Why didn't you try it?" he cried.

"What with?" grunted Reno.

The blackened face of the other man assumed an odd bluntness and all the two hundred beefy pounds of the man teetered to a crouched position. After a long pause he let his gangling arms go lax. "I've made a mistake," he observed shortly.

"You made your first mistake in Blackrock the other night," pointed out Reno.

"You'll not be improvin' your chances by sayin' that to me," breathed Wolfert.

"I should play it humble?" asked Reno. "No, that won't do. You're not fool enough to believe I'd cave in at this stage of the game. I don't know what this is all about but—"

Wolfert's broad and challenging face hardened. He rapped out swiftly: "Oh yes you do! You know damned well what it's about."

"Let it go like that then," Reno responded. "Your second mistake is right here. I don't care much about bein' slugged and kicked around."

"There'll be no more mistakes," growled Wolfert. "Get your horse."

Reno let the talk drop. A sweeping reaction took hold of him and the ache in his head ran through the rest of his muscles, leaving him faint and dispirited. It was a real effort to get into the saddle and wheel around. At Wolfert's gesture, he crossed the glade and passed between the great, virginal pines; and presently hit a sunless trail that looped downward. Thus by degrees they descended from the hill country proper and entered the more open folds of the bench. Going over a meadow marked by sagging rail fences, they entered a thicket of willows, forded a shallow creek asparkle with sunlight, and then pushed into a wider and more gentle clearing studded by the aging and decrepit Benton houses. There seemed to be no life about these, but when they drew abreast the porch of the main house a whip-figured little man appeared and stood attentively by.

"Put him in the back bedroom," said Wolfert.

Reno walked through the doorway. Nor did he pause in the shattered front room, but instead went on along a hall to its end and turned to the left and through another doorway. When he swung around he found the little man studying him with a round curiosity. "Seem to know your way about," said the fellow.

Reno only shrugged his shoulders, yet he realized he had made a mistake. The little man opened his mouth to speak, changed his mind, and closed the door. Reno stood a long while in the center of the room, hearing the other walk back to the front of the place. Meanwhile, his eyes traveled from wall to wall, from the scarred floor to the water-stained ceiling, and his features darkened and grew more embittered. Here, in the bygone years, he had lived and slept and played as a child. The room had been warm then, and the cheerful spirit of a fine home life had made his boyhood seem like a long holiday. This ruin now staring him in the face hit him hard; it was the last outrage, the final bit of desolation and sacrilege. There was a shapeless bunk in one corner and a rat-eaten mattress on it. Going over, he sank full length, face downward.

"Old times," he muttered, "come back."

He fell asleep, never realizing how greatly the wear and tear of the recent hours had drained his vitality. When he woke it was with a quick tensing of muscles, with a sudden shock. The room was full of shadows, and there was the sound of many men talking in the front part of the house. Turning half over he saw the little man crouched beside the bed, a queer, catlike look of absorption on the thin and evil cheeks. At Reno's abrupt rise, the little man swung alertly back.

"Brother," said he, admiringly, "you sure let the cares of the world go to hell. I could've shot a cannon over you, unbeknownst. Feel some better?"

Reno was astonished at the change in himself. He had come to this room miserable in mind and body. Standing erect now, he felt the old freshness of spirit course through him like fire. He was sharp-witted again, full of hope, sure of himself. But all he said to the little man was: "What time is it?"

"Towards evenin'," said the little man. "Not that it should make any difference to you. You're wanted out front."

Reno went through the door and down the hall. The little man followed with a covert warning. "Mind your talk. Wolfert's on the ramp." Then Reno came into the front room and paused to find himself bracketed by the eyes of eight or ten of the hardest, most lawless faces he had ever seen.

A fire burned in a tin stove, and a lantern on a center table threw out an uneven light, only half touching those figures posted around the walls. The talk ceased on the instant. A treacherous silence rushed across the room; Reno, reaching for his tobacco, saw them congeal, saw their cheeks take on a smooth expressionlessness. It was as if he had challenged them by his appearance. Certainly they were on guard—the lack of outward emotion was clear indication of that. But an excessive and brooding interest lay in their eyes—an interest that was tremendously hostile and abidingly suspicious. Running his own glance around, Reno found Wolfert posted in a remote corner; and Wolfert, finding himself spotted, suddenly broke the spell.

"Well—anybody ever see this man before?"

Silence came again, increasingly weighted with sullen antagonism. Reno, feeling the oppression of it, lit a match to his cigarette, the blue glance narrowing across the point of flame.

"Skinny—you ever see him before?"

The little man who had acted as messenger came from behind Reno, slowly shaking his head. "No, Hale. I ain't ever."

Another hand broke in. "If he's somebody we had ought to know, who is he?"

But Wolfert walked to the center of the room. "Nobody," he rapped out. The blackened face went questing along the walls, rankling anger printed on it. "I've got to ride. This fellow goes with me. Skinny, get his horse. Put out that fire and put out the lamp. Everybody stay close at hand till I get back. Keep ridin' the edges of this clearin', but don't let me catch any of you strayin' beyond bounds. Hear that? And if there's any smell of trouble up in the trees, don't go after it. Drift away to shelter and wait."

"What're we here for?" asked the inquisitive hand.

"Never mind," warned Wolfert. "Don't try anything until I say so. It's my game we're playin'. Come on, Reno."

Reno followed out, glad to be away from that room. He swung up, fell beside Wolfert, and matched the other's easy canter across the clearing. Through another belt of trees, they came to the crest of the bench and saw all the vast prairie below fading away beneath the dark. Over in the west Blackrock's lights began to glitter and wink. Wolfert spoke.

"Reno, except for one thing, you'd never have left that house again. I'm telling you that. Bear it in mind, because you've got to play with me the next couple of hours or I'll smash you in your tracks."

"What seems to be your trouble now?" asked Reno, dryly.

"Vilas wants to see me—and you."

"Me? How does he know I'm in your hands?"

Wolfert's answer came back with a throaty savageness. "I'd like to know that myself. The fact's got to him—and he wants to see you. Now listen to this. You are going to keep your mouth shut. Answer his questions, but under no consideration offer any free information. Get the idea?"

"I get the idea."

Wolfert turned in the saddle. "I thought you would. You're nobody's fool, and I'm not deceivin' myself about what you've picked up the last twenty-four hours. I ain't askin' how much you've stowed away under your hat. I don't give a damn. Nor will I tell you how to handle yourself in front of the questions Vilas shoots at you. I don't know what he's got in his system, either. Take care of yourself the best you can."

"You're coachin' me," reflected Reno, "as if I was on your side of the fence. You know better, Wolfert. Why should I do a string of lyin' for you?"

"Make a break in front of him," promised Wolfert, "and I'll see you dead."

"Might be a hitch in that."

"Wait a minute," interposed Wolfert. "There's another angle to it. You're playin' your own game, too."

"Maybe," admitted Reno. "But that's got nothin' to do with you."

Wolfert said nothing for a half-mile or better. They swept off the last roll of the bench and lined out toward Blackrock straightway. Then the Vilas foreman fell to a milder speech. "Yes, it has. You be reasonable with me and I can put you on to something you want to know. A promise?"

"I wouldn't tie up with you for a million dollars," grunted Reno. "Not with your brand of crookedness."

He thought he had stretched his luck pretty far, but Wolfert seemed strangely anxious over the coming interview; and he remained insistently mild. "Not askin' you to tie up with me. The deal is only to cover what happens in front of Vilas. Your promise don't hold beyond that. I can get along without you afterwards. As far as I'm concerned I'll be through with you and you'll be through with me."

"Free to play hide and run again, that it?" queried Reno.

"Just so."

It was an ironic thought. Reno chuckled. "Your friend The'dore would thank you for the dicker, Wolfert."

"Never mind," cut in Wolfert. "I'll handle that."

"You're pretty sure of yourself," said Reno. "But it's a bet."

"Good. In front of Vilas I'll do all the talking. You stick to yes and no answers. And here's the one thing I don't want Vilas to know—that I'm friendly with The'dore. You were in that scrap last night. All right. Remember that it was the McMurtree boys who started the shootin'."

"Agreed."

Wolfert said abruptly. "Here's my part of the bargain. You ask Vilas what time it is."

"What's that?" demanded Reno. But Wolfert had no more to offer. He closed up like a trap, spurred away at a faster clip. Reno, temporarily in the rear, experienced an odd sensation in his brain. Something long ago forgotten moved out of memory's dead lumber and was alive again. He swore under his breath, laid the tip of his rowels across the pony's flanks, and shot on. The compact stung his pride. Even though it had been made at the point of force, it was something that belittled him to himself, made the future even more complicated. The whole affair was increasingly tangled with the gray threads of deceit and lust and evil; and he stood at a point from which he might survey the uneasy relations of all these men in the worst light. Nothing was clearer to him than the fact that no one of them could be trusted beyond the necessities of the moment. Wolfert, the strongest and most brazen, mirrored the rest in his ruthless and contemptuous attitude of dog-eat-dog. Reno had no illusions concerning the man. Wolfert was now using

67

him. When his usefulness was ended Wolfert would get him.

Blackrock's lights came out of the desert to meet them, and the outlines of the houses broke through the desert shadow. Wolfert curled about the town and advanced on its southern side. Dismounting in the gloom of an abandoned shed, he waited for Reno to come along. Of a sudden his voice was metallic and domineering.

"By God, Reno, you go through with this!"

"I'll carry the interview through," said Reno indifferently. "After that, Wolfert, I'll be looking out for myself."

"What's the meaning of that?" challenged Wolfert.

"Why, you damned fool," retorted Reno, "do you think I was born yesterday?"

Wolfert let out a deep gust of air and said: "All right. That's the way it is. Come on."

He walked straight into the blankness of the building shadows, and Reno felt a touch of surprise at the big fellow's lightness of step. Wolfert's knuckles tapped gently on a wall; after that a door opened to let out a rectangular yellow glow. Peter Vilas' tall frame strode across the light and vanished. Then Wolfert went in and Reno followed, closing the door behind. This was again the room behind the saloon bar; Vilas stood in a corner of it, the Yankee face shrewdly, noncommittally set.

There was a considerable interval of silence, and Reno felt a sort of deadlock between the other two. Wolfert stood across from his chief, the great shoulders rolled forward in an attitude of half defense. He was quite evidently waiting out Vilas, not sure of what was to come.

Vilas said quite unexpectedly: "Hale, where did you get Reno?"

"Found him scoutin' the country this mornin'," said Wolfert cautiously. "So I took him to camp."

"Why?"

"I told you the other night I don't trust him. Who told you I got him?"

But the foreman's question failed to be casual. A deep, sulky resentment was in it. Vilas grinned. "You'd like to know that, wouldn't you? Didn't figure I had my ears cocked that far up in the hills."

"If you got no faith in me," snapped Wolfert, "I'll roll my beddin' and go."

"Don't be such a blasted jackass! Well, I'm waitin'. What happened?"

Wolfert eyed Vilas with a dull regard. "Trouble. The McMurtrees are gettin' ambitious. When we come to get the beef they shot us off the slope. That's the end of that business, Pete."

"McMurtree started the shooting?" broke out Vilas, all his features growing pinched. "McMurtree did?"

"Yeah. I told you that game couldn't last."

Vilas said explodingly: "What took you so long in comin' to tell me?"

"I've been all day roundin' up the boys. They were scattered all over the map. The McMurtrees ain't quit lookin' for us yet."

Vilas had no immediate answer, but he kept staring at Wolfert until the latter's dark face changed. "What are you going to do about it?" demanded Wolfert. "Sit and take it? Or go clean that country out?"

"Leave that to me," said Vilas. "What was your idea about Reno."

"To keep him where I'd have my eyes on him," grumbled Wolfert. "I don't trust him. What you want to see him for?"

"To be blamed sure you didn't get hasty," said Vilas. "The man did me a favor, and I don't intend to have him hurt."

"You want him roamin' around the country, knowin' what he does?"

"Depends on what he knows," answered Vilas. "Wolfert, go out front and bring George here."

Wolfert went to the inner door and had opened it

when something occurred to him. He looked back swiftly. "What's that for?"

"I'm going to start the ball rolling. Get George."

Wolfert nodded and went on, closing the door behind. Almost instantly Vilas turned on his heel and walked to the little table in the room. He pulled out a drawer, took a .45 from within, and shoved it across the table's top. "That's yours, Reno."

Reno reached for it, puzzled. Then his hand snapped back and his eyes hardened against that gun, the butt of which held a star and crescent of pearl. This was the weapon he had taken from the dying Two-Bits.

"Where did you get that?" he demanded.

"Recognize it, do you?" drawled Vilas. "Thought you would. Never mind how I got it," said Vilas. "Shove it in your holster."

Reno's mind recoiled from one growing suspicion— that he was framed; deliberately he pulled away from the thought, knowing it made no difference. The possession of a gun answered all arguments. His fingers closed about the butt. He snapped open the cylinder, satisfied himself as to the loads, and shook the cylinder into its seat. Vilas' face had changed again and now carried a look of bitten purpose about it. All the surface show of good humor had gone. Reno dropped the gun to his holster. "What for?" he asked.

"You know what Wolfert would've done to you?"

"Yes."

"Well, here's your answer. When he comes back, it's your say-so."

"Vilas," said Reno. "I've run a lot of errands lately, but I draw the line on hirin' out as a killer. He's your foreman, not mine."

"Never mind. When he sees you've got a gun—"

Reno broke in. "Lost your faith in him, Vilas?"

"I was wonderin' how long it would take him to figure out this trick," muttered Vilas. "It was in the cards."

"I've got a message for you," said Reno. "McMurtree told me to ask you to draw out of this mess. He can't

70

stop his men from raisin' hell. Maybe you can stop yours."

"One of Wolfert's boys fired the first shot?"

"All of Wolfert's boys fired first," amended Reno dryly.

"I thought so. Well, they'll never be stopped till Wolfert's stopped."

He was studying Reno with a slanting shrewdness, his own secretive purposes lending a hooded quality to the brilliance of the sharp eyes; and returning the stare, Reno understood he was being played for a puppet again. He thought then of another thing. Backing to a far corner, he took a stand. "What time is it, Vilas?"

"Towards nine," said Vilas and reached for his watch. The movement of his arm pushed aside his coat front, exposing the heavy length of chain looped through a vest buttonhole and caught there by a cross-bar of gold made in the form of a steer's horns. Tipping the watch in his palm he announced the time: "Half-past nine. Why?"

Reno started to speak, the words as dry as crackling paper. "Vilas, you're—"

But he was cut off by the opening of the door. Wolfert came in alone, closed the portal behind him. "George is down the street somewhere," he explained. Straightening around he looked first at Vilas, saw something in the old man's face, and whipped his big body flat against the wall. His attention flashed to Reno. He saw the gun —and his cheeks went still.

"Hale," said Vilas with a slurred softness, "you're a cheap crook and never did own brains enough to fool me. I've called you."

Wolfert said slowly: "You've walked into your own trap, Pete. Look close at that man. He was a little kid when you saw him last. Why, you damned fool, there's the son of Hi Benton back to find out who shot and killed his dad sixteen years ago. You're smart, Pete. Yeah, very smart. He's lookin' at you."

6

The End of a Man

Backed against the wall, the man who had been Jim
Reno now became Jim Benton in one sweep of changing
circumstance. All the old fences he had built up around
Jim Benton fell away, all the safeguards and screens he
had hidden that man with turned useless. Something
upset inside him during that fractional minute of be-
trayal. The even balance of his mind tipped; and the
last dissenting scruple at bloodshed died there in the
hushed suspense that began to grow intolerable. He had
sworn to himself that he would never resume his true
identity until he found the killer of his father; and here
and now that purpose apparently was at last answered.
No reason was left for carrying on the false name; and
he saw that even if he wished to continue as Reno he
could not. He stood exposed to these two people and
presently would be exposed to all the desert and all
the hills. The energy of his body flooded along his arms
and through his hand—and left the rest of his muscles
inert and helpless. In effect he became a machine of
destruction set on trigger tension, waiting for the impulse
that would release the dammed rage and drive him into
gunplay. For it was clear to him now that the pair could
never afford to let him go. Whatever their own quarrels,
they would unite in the one effort of getting him.

Wolfert seemed actually at ease, as if he enjoyed
watching Vilas suffer. And there was no doubt of the
cattleman's profound shock. The sly, sharp features went
pallid, the nut-shaped head sagged; and the scheming
eyes flashed out a wildness akin to the desperation of
a trapped beast. Then he made the effort of pulling

himself together. He straightened, said thickly: "You're Hi Benton's kid?"

"Yes," droned Benton. "I'm the Benton kid that drove out of the country sixteen years ago with his mother, in a borrowed wagon and ten dollars of charity money."

Vilas said something strange. "How's that mother of yours? I always wondered about her, poor soul."

"She died six months ago. That's why I am here. You've had a long breathing spell, Vilas. But it's over now."

"Look here, boy," said Vilas, a little more sure of himself, "why talk that way to me? I'm the man that lent your mother the wagon and the ten dollars. You're barkin' up the wrong tree."

"What time is it?" demanded Benton.

Vilas started to reach for his watch, then went rigid again, one finger hooked around the chain. "What in hell—"

"That gold longhorn charm you carry," said Benton evenly, "belonged to my dad. You're pretty raw, Vilas. Must be fifty people around Blackrock who know about that charm."

Wolfert broke in sardonically. "But not fifty people that gave a damn what happened to Hi Benton, my friend. Or could afford to take issue with Pete here even if they did care. Anyhow Pete always was fond of souvenirs. He gave you another souvenir—which is that gun Two-Bits owned."

"Wait a minute—wait a minute," pleaded Vilas. "If it's the charm that's worryin' you, Benton, I can damn soon explain it. I bought it off a puncher five years ago."

"Bought Two-Bits' gun also, I reckon?" queried Wolfert, more and more jeering. "You don't lie well, Pete, because you never had to practice the trick."

Vilas almost shook his fist at Wolfert. "*You* know where that gun came from, you hound! You stole it from Benton's saddlebags the other night and brought it here!"

"What should I steal it for?" rapped out Wolfert.

"Maybe you like to collect scalps!" cried Vilas. "Don't

pull the wool over my eyes! *I* can guess who killed Two-Bits and I can guess why!"

Wolfert's single word was flat and toneless. "Why?"

"To bring on the war again," said Vilas, "and feather your own nest. I told you there wasn't an idea in your head I couldn't read."

"You've got Benton to answer now," said Wolfert.

They turned on him and Benton saw the anger and the heat go out of their faces, replaced by a dragging worry. The oppressive, calculating silence came again, and he could feel the weight of their thoughts. The quarrel had revealed little that was new to him; rather it had clouded his certainty, pushed him back once more into the tangle of treachery and cross-purpose. A moment ago the issue had been clear cut and his own decision made; now he was not so sure of Vilas' guilt.

Vilas shifted on his feet and carefully raised a hand to wipe a damp forehead. The gleaming shrewdness sprang into his eyes again, and he began to talk in a smooth, persuasive manner.

"Look here, Benton. Use your judgment. I've played this game a good many years and never made an error. I hire men to do my chores. I don't do 'em myself. Why should I? All those hands working for Wolfert are really working for me. Wolfert's fetched and carried going on twenty years. Figure that out. I never killed your dad. There wasn't any reason I should. He'd been busted soon enough, which was all I wanted. But Wolfert got to thinking that the easiest way was to knock him over. Wolfert did that."

Wolfert's swarthy features showed a plain cruelty, but he held his temper back and only said: "You're carryin' that watch charm, Pete, not me."

"Take it or leave it," said Vilas, directing his words at Benton. "Now what are you going to do about it?"

"Where is your gun?" asked Benton.

The cattleman's answer raced back across the room. "I don't carry a gun."

Benton swung his attention to Wolfert. "Then it seems to be you and me."

74

Wolfert's shoulders rolled forward and he visibly settled. "What's that mean? You want to call the number right now?"

Benton shook his head. "Not this time. I'll pick my own ground when we go to the smoke, Wolfert. I'll see you in the hills. I'm getting out of Blackrock—now."

But Wolfert's manner shifted and the blocky jaws came together stubbornly. "No."

"You want it here?"

"Right here," grunted Wolfert, and cast a swift side glance at Vilas. Vilas got that warning, and his reply was to turn himself more squarely toward Benton. At the same time he took a backward step, placing Wolfert so much the more distant from him. And as he did so, Benton realized the cattleman had lied about possessing a gun. Both of them were going for him.

"All right," he said evenly. "Let 'er flicker."

"I'm out of it," called Vilas.

"You lie," retorted Benton. "You've got a gun under your left armpit."

Wolfert looked like he was about to spring; his heavy lips were thinned against each other and a pale streak deepened on either side of his nose. "Call it," he rasped.

"Your party," Benton told him quietly.

"I'm out of it!" shouted Vilas, and deliberately turned his back to Benton. He had weakened at the last moment. Wolfert started to curse; his elbows crawled higher and the fingers of his right hand began to spread apart. But Benton was watching the man's eyes, and he saw something in them that defined the next step for him. He said: "I'm going to slide to the back door and go out of it, Wolfert."

"You'll never touch that knob," warned the Vilas' foreman. "I—"

"What's that?" interrupted Vilas, making a full turn. A tray fell in the saloon with a banging noise and a table went over. Somebody shouted, "The eastern end of the street!" at the top of his voice. After that those in the saloon stampeded for the front door. There was a shot, a lone shot that sent a flat echo across town, and then Benton heard the rush and pound of horsemen storming into Blackrock. The saloon building shook with the reverberation; a man's boots made a barren clatter through the now deserted barroom, and in another moment the intervening door was knocked open, to show a lithe young man standing breathless on the threshold. He had no hat, and the color of excitement stained his neck a turkey red.

"Vilas—hey, Vilas, it's the McMurtrees! I saw 'em a quarter-mile down the road—"

The rest of his talk was overwhelmed by a long and detonating blast of gunfire. Without trying to finish his warning, the young man threw himself violently about and raced away.

Wolfert's hand rose from its long fixed position, and Benton saw the fellow's eyes mirror astonishment.

"Why," said Wolfert, "I told The'dore tomorrow night—not tonight!"

Vilas looked at the foreman, only looked. Then his turning arm came against the table lamp and swept it to the floor. All this happened so rapidly and was so confused with those other bits of action within the room that Benton's reactions were delayed. The light went out, or seemed to. At any rate the room went dark, relieved only by the glow coming through from the barroom. Vilas yelled, "You everlastin' fool!" and sprang through that door at the same moment Benton dropped to all fours. The things happened at once. The room flooded with the beat of Wolfert's gun opening up, and the smashed lamp caught fire, the flame rising and racing along the path of the spilled oil. As he fell, Benton dragged the table with him for shelter, but this fresh light in the room laid him wide open, and he knew he had no choice of chances. Wolfert's bullets went high, screaming through the flimsy walls beyond; and then the general crash and batter of the McMurtree attack drowned out all else. Righting himself, Benton came up from behind the table with his own weapon blasting a cover for him. But he had no need of it. Wolfert was gone. Wolfert had retreated into the barroom.

Benton made no more mistakes. Reaching behind, he opened the rear door and stepped into the dark, the next minute hurdling all the junk piles on the backside of the town. He reached the horses, took his own by the bridle, and led it away, paralleling the building line. A hundred yards to the east of the saloon, he left the pony to its own devices and himself went down an alley at full run; at the main street he halted and crouched in the shadows, a spectator watching the storm.

There was no doubt of the fighting rage of the Mc-Murtrees. Their first attack had carried them all through the street and out the far end; they came back now at a rush, massed two and two, firing to either side. Window glass fell on porch top and sidewalk like a jangling rain; the whine of lead ripping across the soft walls rose higher. From his covert, Benton saw light after light go out. The McMurtrees were shouting from point to point, emptying the street, breaking whatever lay before them. They abandoned their compact arrangement—Benton guessed they were feeling the tide go with them—and began to cut through the alleys in pairs, to ride into the stores. The taint of burnt powder drifted along the dark; muzzle flashes made weird glows. Once he thought he saw The'dore in this mad tangle, but a second glance revealed another McMurtree.

Meanwhile, Blackrock began to rally; the opposition strengthened and appeared to collect at the saloon. A McMurtree fell out of the saddle in passing that point; another hill man's horse dropped from beneath him. Seeing that, the McMurtrees began to draw back into the deeper darkness. Benton thought they had had enough and were retreating—and the same thought moved a few of the Blackrock citizens into the street again. But it was a mistake. The McMurtrees hurled themselves into the semilight once more, the head of the column going like the point of a spear toward the saloon. The volleying blazed and crackled, and then there was a resounding crash of horseflesh and wood as the McMur-trees struck the saloon at window and door and literally broke through. Benton, absolutely struck in his tracks, shook an astonished head. He had never seen men battle like this before.

"Must be years of bitterness behind that," he muttered.

He saw now, casting a glance further into the shadows, a lank figure rise from an alley and begin to throw bullets into that struggling mass by the hotel. And presently this man walked boldly into the street, refilling his gun; as he crossed a beam of light, he stood identified —Peter Vilas coolly taking up the scrap. Vilas snapped his cylinder shut, raised his gun with an amazing coldness of nerve. Benton never heard the shot, drowned as it was by the torrent of sound all about him, but he did see the gun kick back in the old man's fist; and he also saw the nut-shaped head nod as if in approval. Vilas tried again, stepped back a few paces, seemed to see some better chance, and pivoted to lay his sights down an alley. But he never dropped the hammer on another shot; instead a gun cracked directly across Benton's right ear and Vilas, raising his face to the glittering sky above him, fell without another gesture. Benton recoiled and snapped his glance along the other half of the street. As he did so, he saw Hale Wolfert rise from his knees— from beside the stable water trough—and cut over the dust. The next moment he was out of sight.

That warned Benton as no other incident could have done. He was between fires, in an alien town that was attacked by men hostile to him. There was nothing left here for him to do. The next move was back to the hills, back to the McMurtree house before the crew got there. This much he had determined in that brief period of crouched watchfulness in the alley. And now he retreated to the rear, got to his horse and climbed into the saddle. Five minutes later he was a mile away from Blackrock, aiming for the bench. From that position he turned to see a long fan-shaped flare of blood-red light sweep skyward. Blackrock was burning.

"And that is the end of Big Lafe's hope of peace," Benton said to himself. "Every man on the prairie will line up to raid the hills and get even. Here comes the war. And that's exactly what The'dore and Wolfert want to see. But I wonder why The'dore jumped the attack on Blackrock up a day, disregarding Wolfert's instructions?" Scowling at the long black outline of the hills before him, he added: "I've about come to the end of the drifting stage. It's time to make a stand for myself."

At the high point of the bench he paused to survey Blackrock again—a great shell of light spreading against the velvet opaqueness of the prairie and the horizon. The town was lost; not all the water in the country could save that tinder-dry collection of frame buildings. It would be nothing but hot ashes by break of day, an insult offered by the McMurtrees for all the past injuries done them, and an insult that would draw the prairie's answer before the passage of another forty-eight hours. Looking steadily at the mark of ruin off there, Benton saw what he had been particularly seeking. The McMurtree outfit, traveling at no great speed, came along the lane of light made by the fire, bound back for the hills. There was, as clearly as he could make out, no party of townsmen following.

He was a half hour in the lead and, continuing the climb, he set a pace intended to increase that advantage. When he reached the comparative level of the long canyon through the hills he laid the pony to a hard gallop, and so came to the plank bridge that had previously betrayed him. This time there was no challenge, and he went along the fog-ridden depression without catching the adjacent house light. Beyond that he began a sightless exploration for the lesser trail, found it, and rose wih another ridge. Two hours or better from Blackrock, he rode into the McMurtree meadow and heard the hound pack come baying forward.

The door of the big house opened immediately. Drawing abreast the porch he saw the girl framed there, her face darkly shadowed.

"Who is it?"

"Me," said Benton, and got down.

A quick expelling breath answered him. Rae McMurtree turned half about and revealed a grave worry. She said rapidly, "Come in—come in, Jim!" And when he passed through, she closed and bolted the door. In this great room the scene never appeared to change. The fireplace rolled out its heat, and Big Lafe stood with his back to it. Jim Benton went over, observing how the recent hours had aged this old man. Heavy lines ran down the fine, swept face, and a shadow that seemed fixed beyond any erasure hovered across his strong eyes. His chin came up but he said nothing at the moment; only watched Benton with a manner that was full of questioning. Rae McMurtree came between the two men and spoke.

"I knew it," she said, and there was a stirring of pride in the words. "He came back before, and I knew he'd be back this time."

"You saw Vilas?" asked Big Lafe, showing anxiety.

"Yes, but it will do you no good."

"He refused?"

Benton shook his head. "He's dead."

Big Lafe stood very still, accepting the news with a deeper show of strain.

"Your boys," went on Benton, "hit Blackrock like a ton of dynamite and wrecked the town. It's burning now. There won't be a solid stick left in it by morning. That ought to be some satisfaction to you, no matter what the consequences."

"We're lost," muttered Big Lafe. "Absolutely lost. The prairie will never let that go by. It'll wipe us out. When it is through there won't be a McMurtree left to tell the tale. My outfit killed Vilas?"

"No," said Benton, thinking it odd how his talk echoed and died in the barrenness of the room. The fire silhouetted the girl beside him, trimmed the squareness of her shoulders and drew out the smooth, calm beauty of her features. She was watching him closely. "No, no McMurtree got Vilas. Call it a matter of justice for once. His own man, Wolfert, shot and killed him from behind."

"Wolfert!"

"It should be clear enough to you by now what part Wolfert plays in this mess. He's high man."

"Why?" grunted Big Lafe. "He's killed the golden goose. He made a profit out of Peter Vilas every time I turned over a herd to him."

"He intends to make more profit with Vilas out of the way. Look here. At the time you met him last night in the meadow he had it arranged. His own bunch of rawhiders were right behind him. Those were the gentlemen that opened up on you. It was his scheme. Don't you see it?"

"He wants a war?"

"He's made one," amended Benton. "Figure it out. While the hill and the desert are tied up in a dog fight he'll go out and rustle the range as he pleases. Who'll get the blame for the stock rustlin'? You will."

"More treachery," said Big Lafe grimly.

"A small part of it."

"And The'dore played into it," growled Big Lafe, anger guttering in his throat. "I tried to hush the boys. They would have nothing to do with me. It was The'dore who cried trouble and took them down there tonight. God blast the man; I've got to put my gun on and settle this for a last time!"

"He played into nothing," contradicted Benton. He fell silent for a moment, feeling the attention of the girl and Big Lafe riveted to him. They were mutely asking questions again, putting their faith in him. But there was something more happening in the stillness of this moment—something definitely happening. These people were leaning on him, they were unconsciously putting the little hope they had in his keeping; he was aware of it with a sort of strengthening fire of energy. It changed his outlook, stiffened him immeasurably.

"I wouldn't say this," he went on, "except that I seem to be one of the parties of the first part now. But The'dore's got his irons in the fire too."

Big Lafe's reply was a halting inclination of his head. The girl, however, vented a quick, accented phrase. "I knew it!"

"When I left here," added Benton, "I walked right into Wolfert and The'dore holdin' a directors' meetin' over near the Benton place. They creased me. I overheard a lot of gossip while they thought I was out. The rest of the story is immaterial. It can wait another day. The point is, The'dore is using the McMurtree boys to keep the fight boiling. Wolfert suggested the raid on Blackrock. The'dore agreed. This is plain—The'dore's all the same as a Wolfert hand."

Instead of lifting Big Lafe to a rage, the news strangely depressed him. His tall frame lost its stiffness and his shoulders drooped forward. "I wish," he said slowly, "I could make the boys see that. But it will never stick. Reno, I'm an old man. I'm finished."

"We'll see," suggested Benton.

"The rewards of a crooked life—and I deserve nothin' better," said Big Lafe dourly.

"While we're on the subject," put in Benton, "my name is not Reno. I am Hi Benton's son. I went away from here sixteen years ago as a little heartbroken kid. But I never forgot the tragedy that did away with my dad and aged my mother. I'm back now to find out who killed the old man."

Big Lafe's quietness of body and manner visibly strengthened. A great fire of teeming emotion poured from the drill-straight eyes—at once relentless and probing. After a long interval he said coldly: "I ought to order you away. Hi Benton was no friend of mine."

"Since you were in the habit of raiding his range when you chose," Jim Benton answered sharply, "why should he have been your friend?"

Big Lafe nodded and held his tongue. It was the girl who answered. "All that is over and we're sorry—though that is poor consolation now. But—have you found out who it was—and not a McMurtree that killed your father?"

"Yes."

"What in the devil's name," Big Lafe muttered, showing something of his old domineering manner, "are you doing here? You've got no reason to put in your gun with me. It ain't reasonable. What's the answer?"

Benton was watching the girl, watching the light of

82

the fire stream across her face and shift its expression. Her lips moved, her hand rose slowly along the rough woolen shirt she wore and paused at the exposed white throat; color stained her cheeks. Benton suddenly looked away, stirred by odd impulses. The girl said calmly: "Never mind his reason, Dad. It may be a good one. I told you I trusted him. I do now—more than before."

Big Lafe came out of his rigid posture, attention running across the room. "They're returning. Benton, help yourself! *I'm* not able to help you!"

"Your horse!" exclaimed Rae, and then ran over the floor. She drew back the bolt, opened the door and slammed it behind her as she hurried out. The hounds were quarreling in the yard. Benton stepped slowly backwards and paused against the kitchen entry, hearing the cavalcade drum along the meadow. Voices, rough and impatient, struck through the walls of the house. Somebody shouted a name. Somebody also distinctly said: "There'll be a guard around this clearin' tonight." Then the girl, breathing quite hard and her eyes ablaze with excitement, came up behind Benton, through the kitchen. Boots tramped over the front porch.

"I led your pony to the woodshed," whispered Rae McMurtree. "What else do you want me to do?"

"I'll take a hand," murmured Benton and backed into the kitchen. The girl, touching him briefly on the shoulder, passed on, closing the door; but Benton, crouched against its kitchen side, opened it again half an inch or so, and thus he saw the McMurtree crew stamp in from the night, full of swagger and full of hard temper. The'dore was foremost. The'dore's cavilling, knife-scarred face sought out Big Lafe, and a queer, suppressed pleasure showed itself around the foreman's lip corners. The'dore stepped in front of the old man, insolently speaking.

"I've done what should have been done years ago. You only talked about doin' it. Lafe, make up your mind to it—I'm boss here now. I'll take charge of the McMurtree affairs. These lads want more than an old man's pipe dreamin'. You're through."

Big Lafe answered in a voice that was choked and trembling. "The'dore, what have you done to my boys? God forever damn your black heart, what have you done to them? Where's the others? Where's the other twelve lads?"

Benton measured the McMurtree ranks with a close interest. He counted nineteen hands in that party, suddenly realized that it had been badly handled in the fight. Only twenty-four hours previously the outfit had filled the hall; now it stood shrunken in the lamplight. Blackrock had taken its toll.

"I have managed this family for twenty years!" went on Big Lafe, almost crying. "For twenty years! And I never led it to slaughter!"

"You've got to fight fire with fire," grumbled The'dore, not quite so forthright in his manner.

"You whelp!" shouted Big Lafe. "It's McMurtree blood you're spillin'—not yours!"

"Blackrock," defended The'dore, "is wiped off the earth."

"What of it? That won't help the lads lyin' dead and deserted down there! The'dore, all the prairie ain't worth the life of one McMurtree! You hear me?"

"Lafe," broke in another man sardonically, "you've lost grip on yourself. The'dore's right. You're too old to handle this scrap any more. If we'd hit back twenty years ago like we hit back tonight, maybe we'd be out there as kings of the country instead of spendin' all this time dodgin' through the trees. Well, we've made a start. We'll cut the mustard too. Quit raggin' The'dore."

The'dore stared at Big Lafe with an ironic grin. "There's your answer," he grunted. "Now let's have no more squawkin'."

Benton heard Big Lafe's breath rush into the stillness of the room. Turning, he went across the kitchen on the balls of his feet and out the back way. Pausing a moment, he scouted the yard and saw none of the Mc-Murtree hands moving around. All of them evidently were inside and taking part in the showdown. Thus reassured, Benton crawled beside the house wall until he arrived at the front porch and then, once more checking the shadows, he slid amongst the horses and quietly began lifting the rifles out of each saddle boot. It was a measure of half security and had nothing to do with the immediate dangers of his position; but he was thinking ahead to the time when he might be forced into the hills again to conduct long distance war against The'dore and The'dore's men. All precautions counted. The fewer guns they had, the fewer bullets would he be ducking. The whole thing was touch-and-go, a seizing of each moment and its chances. He made two trips to the brush to hide the rifles, and after the second trip crawled back to the front porch and laid his hand on the latch. One man was talking arrogantly, and the voice tones rumbled and crackled around the barrack-like spaces of the room.

"Time to do something on my own account," Benton told himself quietly, and pushed the door open.

It was The'dore who talked, and the unnecessary strength of his words cloaked the lesser sounds of Benton's entrance. He closed the door behind him and stepped sidewise, alertly watching the row of backs presented to him. Only Big Lafe and the girl commanded his entry, but Big Lafe seemed not to see him. It was the girl's eyes that lifted, touched him, and fell slightly away and swiftly. The'dore said:

"There'll be a guard posted tonight, Lafe. Make no mistake about it—the Blackrock bunch will pay us a visit. We'll be ready to receive them, and what we didn't do down there we'll finish up here. I've got it worked out. I'm going to lay two big brush piles to either side of the meadow and drench 'em with coal oil. When that gang does come stormin' along I'll have these brush piles lighted. They'll be caught between the firelights."

Benton lifted his gun. "Wait a minute," he said conversationally.

He was afraid of that first moment of shock and astonishment—afraid that these men might react to the instant's warning and knock him out of his tracks. And for that reason his phrase had been gently, casually pitched. But as it was, they came around all at once, and he thought he had lost his battle then and there. Those lithe riding bodies wheeled and swayed, and he saw arms drop lower and lower. Eyes flashed blackly at him. Tense antagonism clamped the dark-tanned features into a common expression that made each McMurtree look increasingly like the others. One man—he was only a boy—seized the butt of his revolver and half lifted it. The'dore, sheltered where he stood, called out angrily: "Get him—go on, get him!" But his words were overridden by Big Lafe's stentorian contradiction.

"Leave him alone! The man has done me a favor!"

Benton rode out the crisis with a cool, smooth drawl. "If I wasn't a friend of you boys I wouldn't be here. Why should I ride into certain grief?"

"Then what's that lifted gun for?" yelled The'dore.

"I wasn't so sure of my reception," murmured Benton.

"Get him!" cried The'dore, so roused that his talk was thick and clumsy. "He's the man that framed that trap—and then ducked out of it!"

"Wrong, The'dore," advised Benton with the same downbearing calm. "I staged nothing. And I didn't duck out. You lads rushed away from me. I've had a tough time finding my way back."

"Where've you been since dark last night?" challenged The'dore.

"Where would you suppose?" Benton parried. He looked straight into The'dore's thin, slashed face, and he saw the sullen eyes widen and contract. Something passed through The'dore's head, something that of a sudden brought his lips together speechless.

At that Benton knew he had breasted the first dangerous wave of antagonism. As for the rest of the McMurtree hands, the long maintained discipline of Big Lafe's authority seemed still to have its effect. They held fast.

"Leave him alone," repeated Big Lafe. "He has done us a favor."

"What favor?" grunted The'dore.

"Let him tell it," said Big Lafe and waved an arm

86

gently at Benton. It was a clear signal that he had done all he could, and that from this point on Benton was the governor of his own fortune. Seeing it so, Benton ventured a shift of position. He moved quietly around the group and toward the fire, keeping his back to the wall. When he stopped he was within fifteen feet of The'dore—commanding the foreman; more than that, he had flanked the other hands and no longer sustained the deployed weight of their possible attack on him. If they opened on him it meant a shifting and an interval of confusion. The'dore got the meaning of that immediately and he started to speak.

"You dumb mugs—"

"The'dore," broke in Benton, "why not let it ride?"

He had the foreman guessing. The'dore's unlovely visage became additionally compressed, and he shifted his weight without stepping out of his position. Benton let the suspense pile up, glad of the respite. The worst lay ahead. Still casual, he allowed the muzzle of his gun to drop, and it hung limp in his fist while he tested his luck.

"I saw the bonfire on the desert," he remarked. "Made a nice little blaze."

"Where were you?" rapped out The'dore.

"On top of the bench," said Benton readily.

"How—" began The'dore. Then he stopped and scowled. "You spent a lot of time foolin' around," he finished gruffly.

"And learned a lot of things, The'dore. When did you decide to hit Blackrock?"

For a reasonable length of time The'dore delayed the answer, apparently reasoning out the question and weighing it. "What difference," he finally said, "would it make to you?"

"It was a day premature, wasn't it, The'dore?"

The'dore's muscles went tight. He swung into a visible crouch. But he disregarded the question. It was one of the McMurtree hands who spoke up, puzzled. "How's that?"

"Attack was to have been tomorrow night," explained Benton negligently.

"Who told you?" pressed the hand.

Benton ventured a brief side glance at them and saw he had the complete attention of the crew. He drew a small breath, pinning his eyes to The'dore. "You've been badly fooled, boys. I don't blame you for wipin' Blackrock off the map. But it ain't your idea, like you think. A cleverer head figured it out. A fellow that wanted a roaring good war started for his own profit. While the desert is chasing you fellows all over hell's half acre, he'll be out stripping the range—and you will get the blame."

The'dore relaxed. The'dore permitted himself a flicker of a smile that was wry and dangerous. "Seem to have the confidence of this fellow, Reno."

"The confidence was sort of forced on me."

"Here," said the McMurtree hand, "let's get somewhere. Who's the man?"

"Hale Wolfert."

"And how," shot out the hand, "would you be wise to this?"

"When the fight came up last night," explained Benton. "I drew out of it. Wasn't my fight. Next day I started down the slope and ran into a pair of gentlemen seriously talkin' shop. I was laid cold. But I heard those two talk plenty. They arranged the attack for tomorrow night. One of those fellows was Wolfert—and he took me to his camp. I finally broke away—and got back here to meet the other man. That crook right there —The'dore."

The'dore's grin of cold fury widened. "I thought you'd mess up some such story."

Benton pressed on, driving his point home. "That fight with the cattle was staged. Wolfert meant it as a starter."

"Yeah?" growled The'dore. "You—"

"The'dore was in that also," snapped Benton. "For proof of it—where was The'dore when the shooting began? On the dead lope, away from the meadow. That first bust of lead found him away to the other side of the cattle. You bet he knew. Any of you recall seeing him in the running scrap that followed? Of course not. He wasn't in it. He never showed up till daylight next morning."

"Who are you?" asked the McMurtree hand with a clear show of thoughtfulness.

"Jim Benton, son of old Hi."

"Oh," muttered the hand. "I begin—"

"Sure. My own irons in the fire. But I've found the man that killed the old boy. It's no McMurtree and so I've no grudge against you. But you're playing the part of suckers. You went down to Blackrock and you lost a lot of men. Where was The'dore during *that* scrap? I didn't see him in the lead—and I was in the alley watching pretty close. Suckers—that's the bald fact."

The McMurtree hand turned slowly to The'dore. "Guess it's up to you to take care of this dude, The'dore."

"I can do it," rasped The'dore. "Benton, just drop that gun."

"I'd as soon see you draw," said Benton, evenly.

The'dore's eyebrows came further down. A squinting concern framed the slitted light of his eyes. He drew half a breath, seemed to hold it. Then he called out to the crew, "Spread across the room. If he lifts that gun—"

Benton, not daring to let The'dore get beyond the focus of his vision, heard the crew slowly break from the compact huddle and obey the order.

"Now," repeated The'dore, "just drop the gun and walk out the door."

Something happened then that Benton didn't quite catch. The girl had apparently left the room a little before. She came running from the kitchen now, and her command was like a dash of cold water.

"No! Get out of here—all of you! March, you fools! The'dore, do you want a load of buckshot?"

It broke the tension and turned all of them in her direction. She stood beside the fireplace, a double-barreled shotgun lifted on her own kin. The'dore swayed forward, but Big Lafe's arm pushed him roughly back. Then somebody cursed violently and wheeled around.

In another moment they were filing out to the porch. Stepping backward to the wall, Benton laid his gun on The'dore, whose attention had wandered. "You, too," he said softly.

The'dore flung up his head. "You'll never leave this house," he muttered. "You never will. Rae, I'll have something to say to you later—when this is ironed out." Afterwards, the echo of the threat flattening against the high beams, The'dore went over the boards, heels dragging, and left the place. Benton waited for that. He kicked the door shut, shot the bolt, and sprang aside. "Blow the light," he called. "Get away from the fireplace."

It was the girl who whipped out the lamp's glow. Big Lafe stood motionless, muttering, "We're no better off. We're worse off. Should have taken their guns."

"We didn't have enough bulge on 'em to work it," said Benton. "You don't get the hang of this business. It's one thing at a time. This was the best we could do—this time."

Part of the crew ran the length of the porch, heels making a clatter. The girl said sharply, "Dad, get away from that fire!"

"Hide in my own house?" thundered Big Lafe. "Never! I—"

The rest of his words were overwhelmed by the thundering roar of a gun's explosion. Glass clattered to the floor. A high yelling began to rise from outside. Big Lafe slowly turned, put a hand to his chest, and bowed his head, the firelight showing the grim despair riding his fine old face. Then he went down as if fighting the collapse with every stubborn fibre in him; went down on his side and stayed there.

The girl screamed, "Dad—"

"It's worse," grumbled old Lafe, "for you two. For me it's better. The rewards of a crooked life. I'm glad to go thisaway. There, honey, stop the cryin'. Benton, you'll have to get her away from here. You can't hold out in here. Never can. Get her away. Only one man

90

could have done this. The'dore. But he did me a favor anyhow. Stop cryin'—"

Posted in the darkest part of the room, Benton saw the old man die. Rae McMurtree crouched over him, sobbing with a stifled agony that cut into Benton like a knife. Beyond the house wall men were running again, and a call went from place to place. Then a voice punctured through the boards.

"Get upstairs, Rae. We're goin' to blast Benton to hell and gone."

7

The Ridden Shadows

After that bitter-spoken warning, talk ceased outside and all Benton heard for a short while afterward was the soft scudding of men's feet running from point to point around the house—as if they were posting themselves to attack. The fire on the hearth was dying, turning to a dull blood glow; Rae McMurtree still sat on her knees before Big Lafe, but she had stopped crying and he saw her little shoulders rigidly framed against the lessening light, her head raised and her eyes fixed on some point above the mantel. Looking up there Benton found the framed picture of a woman—a wistfully featured middle-aged woman who seemed to survey the room with a profound sadness and wisdom. Benton guessed it to be the girl's mother. But this reflection was brief and hurried. Time went on, the waiting silence of the yard was oppressive and full of threat. The voice called again, more peremptorily:

"Rae—get upstairs! Get out of the room and stay away from Benton!"

"Come away," said Benton gently.

The girl got to her feet and came over to him very slowly; and he was surprised to find how contained her face was; it was as if she had exerted her will to put the tragedy behind her, and it struck him that suddenly she looked a great deal like that older woman whose picture was on the mantel piece—sad, yet resolute and not afraid. Benton expressed the only reassurance he could think of and knew that he spoke clumsily.

"He was a tired man, your dad. Mighty tired. And

he said he was glad to go this way. I'd take his word for that, Rae."

"I believe that," whispered the girl. Then she raised her dark glance to him. "The McMurtree women have always gone through this, Jim. Always have cried over men who died in violence. Disappointment and heart-break and a life of uncertainty in one wild land or another. Before my mother died she told me to expect it—to learn to smile when there was nothing to smile for. There is a strain of lawlessness in the McMurtree blood that nothing will cure. Nothing but a bullet. All this—I knew it would some day come. But I never thought a McMurtree would ever die at the hands of his own kind. Jim, I've been a good soldier till now. Never saying much because I understood how much my father wanted peace to come. But I can no longer feel sorry for what happens to the boys. I'm all through with that."

"Any brothers of yours out there?"

"No. The closest kin I have in that yard is a second cousin. The rest are even less related. The'dore—he is no relation at all."

"I wanted to know," said Benton gravely. "I've got to fight back. It'll be your own people I'm throwing lead at."

"Go ahead!" said the girl with quick energy. "There is nothing more I can do. They are out to destroy and be destroyed!"

"It's me or them," Benton added, wanting to make the point very clear.

She lifted her eyes so that he could see them and she said: "You ought to know how I feel about that, Jim. Do I have to say it any clearer?"

"No," muttered Benton, all at once full of anger and hope. "But I wanted to know it. Otherwise I would have crawled out of here, without shooting."

"You'll never leave me behind," she answered, shaking her head. "I can't trust them any more. I have no place with them. They're wild. They think as The'dore thinks.

And I am afraid of The'dore. I have always been afraid of him."

That cold yonder voice passed through the broken window again. "We're opening up at the count of ten. Are you in the clear, Rae?"

"Go upstairs," whispered Benton. "I'll follow in a minute."

"Watch out," said Rae McMurtree, and held her position. But Benton turned her about with his hands and pushed her away. There in the blackest corner of the hall, he saw her climb the stairs and pause at the head of them. At that, Benton moved. He catfooted along the wall, came beside the broken window, and crouched. Somebody outside issued a suppressed phrase: "All set?" And a man further off repeated it. A moment later a body leaped to the porch and across it. The man at the window flung his cry into the night.

"All right!"

It was the signal for a rising roar of guns, a rending sound of wood and the splintering of glass all about the room. Lead crushed the floor at Benton's feet. Lead whined and whined and flattened against the stones of the fireplace, and the embers of the fire leaped up as one bullet and another tore into it. Benton stiffened himself, catching the silhouette of a McMurtree hand wavering outside the window. He lifted his revolver and waited with a congealed patience till he saw his target fair and sure; then he fired. That man went down, never saying a word. But beyond a thick, savage shout broke through the detonations.

"Go after him—go after him! Smash that door down before he kills anybody else! What's the matter with you yellow mugs?"

That's was The'dore, speaking from shelter. Benton wheeled and ducked away from his location. He had been spotted by some hand shooting from another window, and the slugs of that marksman rapped the flooring right at his heels. Once more flattened against the wall, Benton studied the windows until he caught the muzzle flash coming through one near the front door. He fired only once, pivoted again, and raced up the stairs to the gallery. They were sledging in that door with a heavy piece of timber.

"Jim," whispered the girl. "We'd better try to get away. The storeroom roof leads off from my bedroom window."

"No horses, no chance."

"Your horse is in the shed just beyond the storeroom."

The end of the timber battered through the panels of the door and jammed there. Benton took a hand rest on the gallery railing and put his last three shells into those panels with a fighting fury that rose beyond all bounds. Savagely pleased, he heard them yelling on the porch, and he knew he had made a hit. The end of the timber skewed upward as the outside part was dropped and deserted. A moment later a fresher and more intense volleying stormed through the windows. Powder smoke wavered toward the ceiling. The girl smothered a cough and laid a hand on Benton's shoulder while he reloaded.

"We had better try it," she urged. "No use trying to hold out here. They'll get in."

"They're in," grunted Benton and leaned far over the rail to command the kitchen doorway. Three men came through it at once, bodies dim in the darkness of the room. They hurtled through, jammed together and firing as they entered. Afterwards they broke, each man advancing on a different tangent, sweeping the shadows for a target they could not see. Immobile for one brief interval, Benton watched—at the same time hearing the front door grind on its hinges again. One arm moved the girl backward, out of range; the other brought up the gun with a dragging deliberation. Benton said: "Up here, boys," and let go. The foremost hand, almost at the foot of the stairway, emitted a great, gusty cry and snapped his weapon around. But Benton pinned him in his tracks, the roar of the concerted explosions washing like waves of water around him. He caught the second man over in the middle of the room, saw him spin and fall; and with still that maddened coolness touching every nerve and fiber, he tried for the third hand ducking back beneath the gallery by the fireplace. This one shot away a section of the stairway banister, knocked up a loosely nailed board of the gallery itself not a foot from where Benton stood. And then, cursing at each hammer fall, he hooked himself around the kitchen doorway's edge and got beyond range.

"The front!" cried the girl. "Watch out!"

But Benton had seen the door go down from the corner of his vision and now, free to divert his attention, he did all that he could do. There were three cartridges left and a doorway full of in-driving McMurtrees. Into that boiling jam of bodies he placed the last of his shots, wheeled, and ran into a bedroom. The girl, preceding him, closed the door quietly and stood speechless in the deeper dark, her breath rising and falling. The booming, excited talk of the ranch outfit overflowed the main hall and beat against the bedoom wall.

"That window leads to the storeroom roof," said the girl.

Benton closed the revolver's cylinder on another load, saying: "It's gone this far. Might as well go a little further. They'll think a long time before they rush those stairs."

The girl crossed the room, pulling aside the curtains. "The window is open. Your luck won't last forever, Jim."

"No," muttered Benton. "It never has."

"Then come on."

He was listening to the unexpected crash out there in the hall. It sounded like an axe knocking away on the stairs. Furniture tipped and was dragged across the floor. One man's voice seemed to be ordering all this in rapid, nervous phrases. In the fore part of the yard a shot exploded. "But," said Benton, "it's better for you to be left behind than to be struck by a bullet meant for me. Crossing the roof is dangerous business, Rae."

She was not beside him. Turning, he saw her slip through the window. A soft whisper came back. "Whether you want it or not, you've got me on your shoulders. Come on."

He followed out, let himself down the two feet to the peak of the storeroom roof, and flattened himself beside the girl, who was full length on the shingles. A solitary figure galloped clumsily out of the barn, passed beneath them and around to the front of the house. Elsewhere, Benton could make out no McMurtree standing guard. Doubling up, he let go of the roof's ridge and worked down to the eaves; and a moment later dropped to the ground. Reaching up, he seized the girl as she came to the eaves and steadied her. She was whispering again.

"Follow me and I'll run straight for the shed where the horse is. It's only—"

"Hold fast!" warned Benton and gripped her arm. A gun spoke flatly across the front yard. A man began crying for the McMurtrees at the top of his voice. The smashing echoes in the house stopped abruptly, and Benton made out the pounding of feet across the living room floor. Hard on that—not more than a full breath after it—the surrounding blackness was pierced by the stinging whine of rifle bullets, and away off at the lower edge of the meadow the trees began to reverberate with flat reports strung together—like the explosions of firecrackers.

"Try it!" snapped Benton. "Got to get out of here now! That's the Blackrock party come to pay back the raid!"

He lost the girl in that space of time it took him to turn around. But he heard her running in the shadows, and he followed more or less blindly till the bulk of a small building came against him. She was waiting there, and catching his arm, she led him around to a doorway and through it. His horse moved up, swung against him.

"Out this door and straight forward," said Rae swiftly. "The trees are about two hundred feet off."

"Down—flat down!" grunted Benton, and he fell, pulling her with him. There was trouble nearer at hand and instantly at hand. The rifles were rolling out a louder fury along the meadow, and from that immediate area beyond the shed—where the girl had indicated their safety to lie—a great clatter and smash of brush announced a flanking attack. He heard men break clear and come on afoot, calling sibilantly to each other; and presently he made out the shifting line as it breasted the dark. Guessing that there were about six in that line, Benton crawled to the sill of the shed door and laid his gun across it. "Roll aside and keep your head low," he muttered to Rae.

He thought the attacking hands meant to collect by the shed. They raced on with every indication of doing it—which meant disaster for him and for the girl. Nothing could prevent discovery, nothing could prevent the excited play of bullets once the discovery was made. Thinking that, Benton lifted his gun to check and throw them back. But before his hammer fell a change occurred. The main body out in front of the house seemed to be halted by the answering resistance of the McMurtrees in the house. A heavy call rode the shadows—a call of warning and direction; and in response the half-dozen hands swinging up to the shed sharply veered and went by it, aiming for the house.

Benton thought, a moment later, that the foreground was clear, and he started to rise when a pair of men came dimly into view, crossing the ground at a slower pace. They disregarded the general fight. In fact they appeared to be avoiding it, for Benton had barely time enough to roll aside from the shed's doorway when those two reached it and stopped. They were breathing rapidly, talking in clipped monotones.

"Damn fool stunt—to hit the front of the house," said one.

"Wolfert's full of fool stunts," grunted the other.

"You in any hurry to run against that shootin'?"

"Do I look like it?"

"We-ell, this is a good place to be."

"Yeah, if Wolfert don't catch us."

"He's plumb busy over yonder."

"Don't lay no bets on it. He's an Indian for findin' out things."

"Say—there's a pony in this shed."

They stopped talking. Benton shifted his gun and held his breath. Such faint light as came through the door opening was blocked out as one of the two men tentatively stepped in and halted. A long, straining moment of suspense ensued. The pony blubbered a little and shifted forward; one of his feet grazed Benton and that seemed to frighten him, for he fiddled backward with an excited blast through his nostrils. The man remaining outside issued a low warning. "I wouldn't be foolin' around, Jeff."

"Somebody," said the fellow inside the shed, "put this brute here for a quick run." He took another step forward, changed his mind and wheeled about. Benton saw him cross the faint shield of the doorway and move beyond it.

"This ain't no place for us," said the first voice. "Too many stray slugs."

"All right. We'll amble toward the barn."

They went away at a trot and their steps finally faded into the general uproar of the fight in the forward meadow. This had reached pitched proportions. All the guns were ripping the darkness into shreds. A stray shot ticked the house corner and came by the shed with a liquid, whistling sound. A man in the meadow was yelling with a crazy ferocity, but nothing he said made sense. Yet it served a purpose; it never varied, never moved nearer or went further away, and from it Benton judged the attackers were no nearer to the house than they had been. The McMurtree fire held them.

What puzzled him most was the disposition of the six that had flanked the shed and had gone toward the side of the house. He heard nothing more of them—not the faintest sound of their maneuvering. Profoundly keyed to the treacheries of this mad hour, he rolled back to the doorway, rose, and stepped outside. When he crawled to the corner of the shed he thought he saw black forms shifting through the lesser black. But he could not be sure. Returning to the shed he whispered his guess.

"Appears to be a break here for us. We'll try it."

She was up and beside him instantly. "Ride out on the dead run, Jim?"

"No, that won't do. You get on your hands and knees and crawl across to the tree line. I'll wait about half a minute and then follow with the pony. If we get separated in the brush I'll call out."

"Jim, I don't want you to—"

He took her arm and pushed her through the doorway. "Run along," he murmured. "I'm still the general of this army. Straight across, on your hands and knees."

He saw her drop and move away, and then he lost her. Afterwards time lagged more intolerably, and he caught himself methodically counting. There was a distinct break in the fight that worried him—a shifting of forces. Wolfert's men—for the talk of the two shirkers had revealed the identity of the party—were coming along the side of the meadow with the apparent idea of hitting the house at an angle. The McMurtrees caught that maneuver and began to fire through the side windows, instantly. The gun reports shifted, clashing out more distinctly, and Benton picked up the whipping of the spent lead along the ground and in the brush. Meanwhile his mechanical counting reached thirty and stopped. Seizing the pony's check strap, he led it through the doorway, paused for a final check, and struck straight across the cleared area.

Suddenly, no preliminary trickle of light announcing it, two great bombs of fire shot into the sky from the fore meadow. The McMurtrees had managed to build their brush piles in that brief period between the death of Big Lafe and Wolfert's attack. It was the coal oil that made those instant spires of light, at once catching part of Wolfert's men in a deadly silhouette. But the light did more than that. It reached around the side of the house, dispelled even the farther shadows, and caught Benton halfway between the shed and the brush. Someone cried out: "Catch that man!" A bullet snatched the dirt at his feet and he saw a pair of hands race for him tandem style. There was only one answer. He went up the wrong side of the horse to the saddle and dug in his spurs. Bent far down he crossed the rest of the open stretch at great lunges and drove heedlessly into the marginal bushes. A volley of shots followed him. The horse abruptly winced and staggered; and as Benton threw himself clear, the beast fell.

Benton sprang aside from the bullet-swept space, shouting: "Rae—Rae!" Then he brought up short, feeling the girl's arm reach out and touch him. For answer he picked her up bodily and ran on into the depths of the timber—a good fifty feet on, down the lip of a gully and into the mushy underfooting of a forest creek. Safe here, he stopped and let the girl stand.

"We've lost a horse," he muttered.

"There's a bunch of ponies back by the edge of the yard," said Rae. "Left there by those men that came toward the shed."

"Wait here," said Benton, and climbed from the gulley. The fires in the meadow were burning fully, and he saw the horses bracketed against this light only a little to the left of him. Closing in, he got out his pocket knife, cut the cinches of all but two, and led these back. He missed the girl again and had to send out a short halloo. When he found her she said:

"This is a warning for us, Jim. We must not get separated in these hills."

Then she swung beside him and waited for him to move.

"What I want to do," reflected Benton, "is get back to the high country where we were riding the other day. You know the trails. Lead out."

"Jim," challenged the girl, a definite ring in her words, "I want to know about this. Are we staying in the hills or are we leaving them?"

"We'll never go—not unless we're driven out foot by foot."

She had no more to say, and he wondered what had prompted the question. But it was a tricky trail she followed, and he lost her twice before she made the long curve about the McMurtree meadow and paused on the edge of the southern canyon. She stopped and

101

turned the horse about, lifting an arm to what was going on over by the ranch. "Jim—I'll never go back there. Never! The ground is saturated with blood. I have nothing left—not one single kin worth saving or remembering. It's the end of the McMurtree ranch."

He had no reply. There was none to make. Those great glares were like funeral pyres. The house loomed up like a fortress and the lesser buildings to the rear were squat and dull crimson. Men were rushing out of one covert into another, and long lances of orange-purple crossed the shadows about the barn. In that brief and final inspection he saw one irregular wave of Wolfert men rush from the barn and stumble forward, converging on the back quarter of the main house. Some of them dropped; the rest went on and vanished from view. The yelling increased, pitching across the meadow with a strangled, muted effect. On the porch he saw the climax of one bitter contest; a Wolfert hand leaped from the darker side of the house to the porch and raced across it just as some McMurtree hand opened the door and came out. There was no parrying. Those two plunged together in a snarling, wrenching body-and-body conflict; and the McMurtree man at last caught his opponent under the arms and forced him back into the house. Somebody raced for the trees, never looking behind him; a Wolfert partisan shot out of the barn with a lighted torch in his fist, got against the house wall without injury, and dropped the torch against the wood. After that he scuttled the length of the wall and passed to the rear. Rae McMurtree drew a quick, hurt breath.

"Let's get out of here! I don't want to see any more!"

"Lead for the high point yonder," said Benton gently, and kept his mouth closed during the next long hour. They dipped into the canyon and out of it. They rose to the summits and passed beneath the rolling banks of fog. The far-off firing dimmed and died, but once, turning to scan the blankness of sky and earth, he saw a widening arc of crimson stain the distant obscurity. The ranch was burning. That grim old fortress of the hills was being consumed as Blackrock had been consumed. In that fact was an omen that vaguely disturbed Benton, yet it was soon crowded out by other and more important considerations. They were scraping the ceiling of the world, and eastward the opaque quality of the night began to break. Another day stood on the threshold. Seeing that, Benton called a halt.

"We rest."

They were in a small, pine-surrounded glade that literally dripped with the condensing mists. Unsaddling the horses, Benton made a bed of the blankets and his slicker. "Roll up, Rae," he said. "We'll get what breathing spell we can." She dropped without protest, exhausted. For himself, he rolled a cigarette and cupped a match in the crown of his hat. Crouched Indian fashion beside the girl, he watched the broad hands of light wedge the horizon—glad to have this long night go, yet finding no promise in the hours coming. The worst of the fight was yet to come—of that he was absolutely sure. Such exits as there were from the hills would soon be guarded. Wolfert would never let them go without a contest. Tipping his head, he saw that Rae was not sleeping. Very quiet in the blankets, she watched him through the twilight and fog mists.

"Jim," she asked abruptly, "what crime could possibly be against you? Why should you, of all men, be running from a posse? I don't understand. You're not that sort of a man. You never could be."

8

The Unrelenting Chase

He sat silent a while, puzzling over his answer. The girl turned on her side, mistaking that silence; and she said rather quickly:

"I don't want to pry into your affairs. Let it go."

"A day might come," he mused, "when my affairs might be your affairs. Is that possible, Rae?"

"Maybe," she answered, just above a whisper. "Maybe, Jim."

He smiled a little, and at once the severe and watchful gravity was crowded out of his face. It became cheerful and reckless. "Many years ago I kissed you."

"We were children," said Rae.

"Still, the recollection is there," he insisted. "Has been in my mind for a long, long while."

"If it meant that much to you," said the girl, smiling back at him, "I don't begrudge it."

"As to this posse business—"

"I told you I didn't want to pry."

"Tomorrow," he said simply, "may never come. We're not out of the hills yet. And I wouldn't want you to remember me as a fellow better than I was—or worse."

"Don't you suppose I have eyes to see, Jim? I have watched hard men, mean men, men without conscience or scruple or the least regard for life. You're not that sort. If you were it would show in the way you carried yourself, in the least act and in the smallest word. When you came to our house the first night I recognized you instantly. And do you know what went through my mind? I wondered, even before I spoke, how the years had treated you. And if the years had changed you—

as they change so many. Well, the answer was in front of me while I wondered. You carried yourself straight. You spoke as if there weren't anybody in the land you were afraid of. You looked directly at my father."

"Thanks, Rae."

"As for the posse—" Her voice lessened, turned wistful. "As for the posse—I guess we all make mistakes. I'm not holding it against you. I wish your back trail was clear. But if it isn't, I don't care. I don't care, Jim."

"I'll say this much," put in Benton swiftly, "it was nothing much—and may turn out to be less. And we'll let it ride like that till the shootin's over."

"What are we going to do?" asked the girl.

He kicked the soft dirt with a boot heel, eyes narrowed at the strengthening eastern light. The smile went away and he was once more cool and hard and competent. "My own mind is made up. But you're with me—and that changes the situation. If you say the word we'll keep right on going. On out of this."

"Where to?"

Something in the question turned his attention directly to her. She had risen to one arm; a somber cloud hovered across the dark eyes.

"It's up to you," he said. "Where would you want to go?"

"To the first town outside this country, I guess," she answered slowly, not showing much interest.

"Hold on. I'm barkin' up the wrong stump. You've got no relatives outside of the hills?"

She shook her head. Benton said, "Well, that's a horse of another color."

"No," she broke in. "I don't want you to take it that way. I'm on your hands now. There's no help for it. But once we get away I can care for myself. The nearest town will be all right."

"What would you do?"

"Work. Any kind of work."

"Don't like the sound of it at all."

Somehow, his words went wrong. She showed a touch of pride and irritation. "I'm no charity case, Jim. I will

105

not be treated like a child or a member of the poor farm."

That brought the slow smile back to his cheeks. He chuckled, seeing the color deepen around her temples. "There speaks a McMurtree," he drawled. "Always touchy and mighty independent."

"Well," she said defensively, "I don't propose to have you thinking I'm on your shoulders for the rest of my life. Not for one minute."

"I could think of worse—" He bit that sentence off in the middle and looked away from her. "Less said now, the better. This is a time for some things but not for some others."

"What did you originally decide to do?" she wanted to know.

"If I were alone I'd never move an inch, Rae."

"Then," said the girl, "that is what we'll do."

"You don't get it," he explained. "I mean I'd make my stand right here and wait out what's coming."

"I understood it the first time you said it."

"I came back to settle a score. I'm not entirely sure it is settled. When Wolfert dies I know it is settled. But that's only half the story. I was born in these hills, Rae. This is my old home. I came back to see what it looked like. I don't want to go away now. This country was meant for me. That ranch down on the bench—I want it."

"I don't see how you'll ever get it—or hold it," the girl reflected

"Never get it if I don't make my stand here and now."

"Wolfert will never let you take the old home place."

"Remains to be seen," said Benton, casually grim.

Rae McMurtree's two hands came together tightly. "Jim, I'd hate to see you—"

"What?"

She shook her head and looked away, lips pressed together.

Benton rose and kicked the cramp from his legs. The mists were sinking into the roundabout canyons and this high peak stood momentarily isolated from the world.

The sky was still full of stars, but the gunpowder grayness of early morning filled it, lightened it, and slowly shifted to a paling blue. Eastward a rose light began to lift. False rain dropped from tree and bush. The two horses were a hundred feet off, cropping the lush grass. The smell of smoke drifted on the slight wind—the smoke of the McMurtree quarters. The girl called Benton back: "We might as well have it out," she said.

Benton waited, finding a brighter glow in the girl's eyes. The color of inner emotion shaded the white and even features; a kind of resolute courage fashioned her features into a square outline.

"Say what you were going to say a little while back," she demanded.

"This is no time for it," he countered.

"When will be a better time?" she challenged him. "If it will not survive bad luck it will not survive good. Are you afraid of that, Jim?"

"All right," he answered, at once rough and direct. "I want you, Rae."

She stood up from the blankets. "You can have me."

"We're not out of trouble yet. We're deep in the woods."

"All the more reason why we should settle this. I want you to know it, whatever happens. Give me credit for a little faith, Jim."

"Good Lord," muttered Benton, coming toward her, "don't you figure I do? Here. You've lived among outlaws all your life. You've had no security and no peace. Now you've got me on your hands, knowing I'm hunted. Rae, it may be a bad bargain."

"I know," said the girl. She reached out and took one of his hands. "But I can't run away from myself. If this is the way it is to be for me, then there's nothing more to be said."

Benton gripped her fingers and then stepped suddenly back. He turned away, saying, "There's a lot more to be said, but we'll not say it now. I'm going to that pinnacle to have a look. Better lie down and rest while we've got the chance."

Twenty yards away, he heard her say something indistinct. When he looked around she was smiling and erect. One small hand rose swiftly to her mouth and then went out to him. "Gamblers sometimes win, Jim!" she called. "But if they lose, they've had the gamble anyhow. Run along."

A little farther along, the curve of the alleyway cut her from sight, leaving him with a strange reluctance and strange misgivings. So pronounced was the feeling that he checked and stood with his attention straining the slow, minor sounds arising out of the morning's primeval calm. Reassured, he went on, found a more or less clear grade, and mounted the rough pinnacle. At its tip the panoramic view of the hills unrolled to all sides. By now the mists had condensed in the lower canyons and ran along them like foaming tides of water. Each jagged and rounded surface of the country lay exposed, running northward to a still greater tangle of ravine and ride and sloping out southward to the prairie. That way Benton spent a long survey, seeking the outline of Blackrock and finding only a dim charmark on the earth. Of the McMurtree ranch he could locate no fragment but he saw a layered column of smoke bellying up from behind a flat-topped butte. The passions of men these last few hours had consumed much. Thoughtfully considering the fact, he realized how hopeless it was to expect a lessening of the chase or a softening of the unleashed antagonisms. There was more to be consumed. Fire never dies till it has eaten away the substance of its own heart.

It was Benton's habit to analyze his fortunes pessimistically during idle spells; and to consider those fortunes not at all when in the heat of actual combat. So now he considered the account to-date and found it dismal enough. From first entry into the country he had been pretty much thrown about. Much of this he had expected, indeed had hoped for. But the duration of that willynilly, choiceless fighting had gone way beyond his expectations. At no time had there been a break, or a breathing spell in which he might choose his own plan.

At no time. Events had rushed him along until now he faced a three-way attack.

That was amply clear. The McMurtrees were against him. Wolfert and Wolfert's band would hunt for him. And lastly there was that new force in the battle to account for—the prairie men. They would assemble on the ruins of Blackrock and march forward.

"Each bunch set against the other," Benton told himself, "and all of 'em set against me. I don't know which way to look first. Wolfert may still be engaged with the McMurtrees. Or one or the other party may have run off. The one mighty certain fact is that the prairie bunch will be coming up this way. They'll tangle with the McMurtrees without comment. Probably they'll do the same with the Wolfert outfit if they catch up. Wolfert himself might talk his way into the prairie delegation, but he could never convince the prairie boys that his bunch of rustlers were on the right side. So it stands—all messed up. Only other clear item is that Wolfert will try to write my ticket before I get a chance to betray him to anybody else. The bystander always gets shot in the brawl, and I'm the bystander."

He whipped his hand to the westward and held it rigid, eyes focusing on a miniature clearing on the side of a ridge about two miles distant. A file of men—not very large—charged across that space and fell into the smother of timber again. Benton's glance ran the edges of that particular tree mass, locating the adjoining clearings; and for a long spell he waited, expecting the party to come again into view. When it did, however, it was very briefly and vaguely in the bottom of a canyon. The course taken seemed to indicate an intention of reaching the summit country that he, Benton, was in.

"Not very many there," he thought. "Part of Wolfert's band split off, maybe. Detachment of the prairie people? No—they'd hang together for the big smash. Or else it is what's left of the McMurtree boys. Likely. The sad survivors of a proud outfit."

It was time to move. His trail was yet fresh in the yielding turf of the hills, and they might cut it and follow. But the presence of this group was a definite sign of other riders in the saddle, of a general shifting of arrangement. The tide moved easterly. Accordingly Benton held his position, running strict and intent surveys along each exposed meadow and burn, whipping up the defiles and notches in the north-south distance. Ten minutes of this produced no results; and a last look to the prairie netted nothing. Impelled then by the sense of time wasted, he left the pinnacle and quartered to its foot.

"If I drift backward," he said to himself, "I gain nothing and lose ground. If I sidestep I keep in touch—"

That was as far as his thinking went. Through the trees and along the bending trail Rae McMurtree's half-scream and half-cry of warning poured shrilly and shockingly and quit on a high note. The effect of it was literally to throw Benton back on his heels; and he hung in that balance till the cry, seeming to be released by terrific force, struck the shaggy silence again. Benton plunged on with his head lowered, boots battering on the soft earth. His hand rose and lowered automatically, and thus he rounded the bend and raced over the little glade, gun lifted and veering around. He had drawn the hammer half back before he saw that he could not shoot. The girl sank to her knees, rose with both hands reached forward. The'dore—the slash-cheeked, sullen-visaged The'dore—stepped away from her and cursed morosely; Benton's arms went rigid as he checked his draw. The girl was aware of Benton's return. The'dore, spilling over with rage, had not yet discovered the fact; all his thoughts were on the girl. He lifted her with a heave of his shoulders, got one arm free, and struck her across the face with a force that knocked her down again. And it was then that his shifting glance found Benton. Instantly The'dore's body stiffened. A wild and vicious and hunted expression flashed across the sulky cheeks and thereafter settled to a fixed mask of incredible hatred.

"Rae," said Benton, fury throbbing in his words, "step aside from him."

The'dore took a step toward the rising girl, clearly meaning to use her for a shield. But he was checked by Benton's veering gun muzzle and Benton's dead, flat command. "Stick to your tracks!" The girl turned to Benton and started to speak, but she saw his gaze riveted on The'dore and apparently understood the danger of diverting it. So, white and trembling, she moved back, out of range.

"The'dore," droned Benton, "you've prowled too long."

"You've got the drop on me," muttered The'dore between his teeth. "I can't draw."

"You want to draw?"

"Give me an even chance at it!"

"Why should I?" snapped Benton. "You've got no break comin' to you."

The'dore's eyes squinted across the interval, red and crafty. His tone turned wheeling and persuasive. "Look here. When you was down and out yesterday morning and Wolfert wanted to finish the job right there, I balked at it. It's me you can thank for bein' alive."

"You're a yellow hound, The'dore," stated Benton. "All that stopped you from putting a bullet in me was a streak of butter up your back a foot wide. You wanted to do it bad enough."

"I didn't do it, did I?" countered The'dore. "That's the chance you owe me."

"What are you on my trail for?" grunted Benton.

"Me? Hell, I'm not on your trail. I'm on my way. I'm leavin' this country. I'm through."

"Why? Seemed to me you and Wolfert had it all agreed. What are you worryin' about now?"

"Wolfert—that dog!" yelled The'dore with an incredible venom.

"So you're not good friends now?" asked Benton ironically.

"I'll kill him!" breathed The'dore.

"For a fact? In other words, my lad, he cut your throat before you had a chance to cut his. I never knew a thief worth trustin'. You're no exception."

"Call this off," pleaded The'dore. "Call it off and I'll be on my way. You got grief enough without scrappin' with me. I'm all through I tell you."

Benton let the talk drop for a minute. The forest stillness flowed through the clearing. Eastward a great glow of warm bright light rose, heralding the sun. A woodpecker attacked the surface of a dead snag above them and long staccato sheets of sound broke the peace. The scent of pine and steaming earth clung heavily to the air. The girl had her back to a sapling, the small shoulders sagging; but her eyes were pinned to Benton with an odd care. As for The'dore, the strain of waiting cut deeper slashes across his lawless visage. He stirred uneasily.

"Reach across with your left hand, pick your gun with two fingers, and drop it to the ground," ordered Benton.

"You're not going to pull a Spanish on me!" bawled The'dore.

"Do as I say," pressed Benton.

The'dore obeyed with a lagging reluctance. He plucked the gun from its holster and dropped it at his feet. Benton smiled grimly. "You're full of tricks, my friend. But that's an old one. Now kick that piece over my way."

The'dore's lips swept to a cruel, vulpine crescent. He caught the gun on his boot toe and sent it spinning. Benton reached down, got it, and flung it into the far bushes. He straightened suddenly, catching a forward gesture on The'dore's part; and for another dully dragging interval he studied the McMurtree foreman keenly.

"Now get on your pony and fog out of here," he said at last. "I ought to use my quirt on your back. But there's some pleasures I guess I'll have to pass up."

The'dore sighed enormously. The strain went from his cheeks and he reached into his vest pocket with a careful deliberation, bringing out his cigarette tobacco. He rolled his smoke, contempt gradually curling into his lip corners. Catching this shift of temper, Benton realized

112

he had misjudged his man. The'dore mistook mildness for weakness, as did all outlaws who lived by force.

"You'll never get in the clear," sneered The'dore. "I'm tellin' you. You never will. This minute the hills are bein' locked up. Damn you, Benton, I wish I was around to see your finish!"

The'dore pulled a match from his pocket and lit it against his thumbnail. Benton, weary of the delay, holstered his gun and ducked his head. "Get on your pony and go. Should I ever see you floating around here again I won't bother about warning you."

He moved ahead a foot and toward the girl. "This seems the best way, even—"

That was his mistake, and he realized it even as he tried to whip himself backward and get his gun in operation again. But he never quite made it. The'dore had been waiting for that off-guard moment. His long body, set for the chance, hurdled the distance, struck Benton viciously, and knocked him back. The'dore's big arms locked about Benton's waist. He tripped Benton and fell with him, and the sheer weight of his body knocked the wind completely out of Benton's chest.

Half paralyzed, Benton tried to roll clear and got a sledging smash on the temple. The'dore cursed and drew up a knee, essaying to grind it into Benton's stomach as he meanwhile reached for the protruding gunbutt on Benton's hip. At that, Benton's breath came back to him with a rush. His arms were free. Lifting them, he caught The'dore about the neck and at the same time kicked the man's body upward with his feet. The'dore emitted a strangled yell and capsized on one shoulder, shaken clear of Benton. Benton rolled and got to his feet and stood there, breathing hard.

"All right, The'dore," he grunted. "I'll get my pleasure after all! Come on up!"

The'dore was at him with a swiftness and a ferocity born of a gamble gone bad. He tried to grip Benton again; but Benton, sidestepping, caught the man with a driving right-hand blow that skewed The'dore's frame half about. Stunned and exposed, he made a fair target, and Benton went for him with a relentless method, ripping the half-mad face fist and fist. The'dore tried to bring his own arms into play. He groped uncertainly, tried for his bear hug. Right then he was wide open, and Benton put the full weight of his body into one mauling smash under the chin. The'dore went down, wind pouring out of his slack and bloody mouth, and rolled agonized from shoulder to shoulder. The deep silence came again. Rae McMurtree ran forward, her hands touching Benton's bruised cheeks.

"Jim—if I'd had a gun I would have killed him!"

"He's through," rasped Benton, reaching deeply for air.

A slow voice said, behind them: "Be careful and don't try to draw."

Spinning in his tracks, Benton saw one of the younger McMurtree boys rise from the brush with a revolver in his fist; and afterwards seven others of the McMurtree clan advanced from the surrounding thicket and closed in.

– 9 –

The Smash-Up

Taken aback, Benton stood fast. But the girl turned
and put her body defensively against him. And she said
angrily: "You fools have made mistakes again. I won't
stand for any more. Do you hear me? If you weren't
blind you'd see the difference between Jim Benton and
that—that killer over there on the ground!" She stamped
her foot and the flushed color burned brighter on her
cheeks. "The'dore led you around like you were a bunch
of infants. He made you jump through circles for him.
You believed in him so much you let my father die in
his own house! Well, what have you got out of it?
Nothing! The house is gone and most of you are gone!
Now The'dore's running away. Do you believe in him
now?"

"Easy-easy," cautioned one of the McMurtrees. "Give
us a little credit."

"What for?" demanded the girl scornfully.

"Yeah," muttered the man. "I know it don't sound
so well."

"What do you want now?"

"The'dore," said the McMurtree bluntly. "We discovered the dope about him last night. We had a showdown. He got away from us."

The fellow holding the gun put it slowly back into
its holster, explaining to Benton, "Didn't know how
you'd act when you saw us come. So we thought it
best to get the drop on you. No hard feelin's?"

"Lin," said the girl, "where are the rest of the boys?"

Lin was the spokesman, a tall and gangling hand with
the pointed and darkish McMurtree features prominently

displayed. He answered slowly. "This is about the size of it, Rae. We're all shot to pieces."

"You can thank The'dore for that!" cried the girl bitterly.

"The'dore," replied Lin noncommittally, "will get his pay, without thanks." He walked over to the fallen ex-foreman and looked down with an expression suddenly bleak beyond measure. He prodded The'dore with his boot and stepped back, waiting. But The'dore was still senseless and after a moment Lin silently motioned to keep watch. Swinging on Benton, he began to speak with a heavy regret.

"You've been on the right side all along. We've been on the wrong. We're glad you got shut of us without hurt and we're sorry it had to happen. You're a damned good hand, mister. I wish—" But Lin McMurtree stopped the wish short and looked about with a sort of wistful hopelessness. "No use cryin'. The damage is done and we're through. We sure have sung our little song. Nothing to do now but pay the fiddlers."

"Where's Wolfert and his bunch?" asked Benton.

"We beat those boys off," grunted Lin with a show of satisfaction. "Just before daylight they got a bellyful of it and raced away."

"Then why," said Benton, "don't you stick it out?"

But Lin kept shaking his head. "It won't do. There's a crowd comin' up the Blackrock-Morgantown road. We sighted it just before we left the ranch. Half the prairie is in that troop. You know what those fellows aim to do, don't you? Sure. Wipe out the McMurtrees for once and for good. They'd do it too, and never let us shout for mercy. I said we had to pay the fiddler, didn't I? We're through. Only thing now is to get out of the country and disappear completely. There ain't any more McMurtree outfit." He looked at the girl, gently saying: "We buried your dad in the grave lot, Rae. It was The'dore that shot him."

The girl nodded and turned away from them, walking back toward the edge of the clearing. Lin said: "Well, this is wasting time. Bring up The'dore's horse and tie him to the saddle. He's goin' with us."

Benton looked at this lank McMurtree and saw The'dore's fate in the man's dark glance. The'dore was through. Then, as if answering the unspoken question, Lin let out a quiet phrase. "He'll get his chance—but he won't deserve it."

Silence fell, full of discouragement and brooding melancholy. They had brought up The'dore's horse and were tying his feet under the animal's belly and his hands to the horn. One of the group mounted and steadied The'dore; the man was waking from his stunned sleep with a painful reflex of his muscles. The scarred face turned from side to side, only half recognizing his situation. He said thickly: "Get Benton—that's the main thing." Then his mind cleared and he looked down at his roped wrists. "You ain't got me yet!" he bawled.

Nobody answered him. His eyes went to Lin McMurtree, full of fear, but McMurtree stared back expressionlessly.

"You think Wolfert's men held together?" asked Benton.

"Maybe—maybe not," judged Lin. "They took a lot of punishment. Ain't so many left as you'd think. I'd hate to go through a fight like that again. It was hell—just plain hell. If those crooks stick by Wolfert now they're bigger gluttons for punishment than I take 'em to be." He bowed his head, quite thoughtful. "You want my straight opinion of it? Well, this country has had a house-cleanin'. In a damned odd fashion. Two crooked sides killed each other off. Ain't that somethin' to laugh over?"

"Boys," pleaded The'dore, begging his case, "if you'll let me go and give me a gun, I'll swear I'll never stop ridin' till I knock Wolfert out of the saddle. So help me!"

He was entirely ignored. Lin looked at the girl, called to her, "Rae, we've got some extra horses. Come along. We're wastin' time here."

She wheeled. "I'm not going with you, Lin."

117

"What?" grumbled Lin. "Lord, you don't think we'd leave you in the ditch—"

"Not going."

"Well how're you goin' to take care of yourself when—" Lin began. But another thought came to him and he pulled his head about and stared at Benton sharply. "So that's it, eh?"

"Yes," said the girl. "That's it."

"What do *you* aim to do?" Lin asked Benton bluntly.

"Stick. This is my country."

"Don't be too proud of your chances, mister. This scrap ain't over. Wolfert's around. And them prairie lads won't consider you very kindly."

Another of the outfit called out, "Harry's comin'."

A slim, small youth spurred up the slope and through the brush. He was hatless and excited. "That Blackrock bunch reached the ranch," he said rapidly, "circled it once and lit out thisaway."

"We've got to tail out of here," decided Lin. "Rae, it's up to you."

"No."

The McMurtrees went to the saddle. Lin looked down at Benton, his face sharpened by that clinging and insistent regret. "I wish you luck. I wish we'd known you a long time ago. One thing I'm damned sure about —you'll do better for Rae than any of her own kin did."

"So long," said Benton.

They moved compactly across the clearing, those ten McMurtrees, with the bound The'dore in the center of the group. Another moment and they were around the trail's bend. Benton heard The'dore lift his voice in a choked, wild-toned cursing; and this continued until the distance dampened and absorbed voice and hoofbeat alike. After that he looked at Rae. "We're makin' a stand," he told her. "But I don't want to make it here."

"You're thinking about the ranch down on the bench," she said.

"That's it."

They went to the horses and stepped up. The girl

118

was watching him curiously. "You realize, Jim, that the sheriff will be with those Blackrock men?"

"I know. But we can't dodge it forever, Rae."

She put out her arm and stopped him. "Jim, I'd rather run than lose you!"

But he shook his head. "That ain't the right answer. Let's go."

She raised her shoulders with a queer gesture of futility and thereafter said no more. Benton left the glade by its sloping edge, tackled the quick-falling side, and reached a canyon's bed. A deer trail went dimly along it, through sedge and little pools made by the condensing mists. They came to a cross-gulch, took it, and by degrees worked out of the high terrain into a lower and more open country. Far behind rose a single shot. The sunlight began to reach between the thinning treetops, and they passed across alternate strips of shadow and golden puddles of light. A vista of the far-reaching prairie opened before them. Seeing that sweep of tawny earth, the girl came out of her abstraction.

"And so I go back to the flats, where I was born. You know, Jim, I never got used to the hills. They were too secretive. Too dark. Too close. They kept cutting off my view. The hills have been a hiding place for my family all this time. I don't want to hide any more!"

"From the porch of my house," said Benton, "the whole world rolls away."

"Jim," said the girl, sharply, "you're not through with Wolfert yet!"

"No," answered Benton. "No, not yet."

The trees made a scattering show and petered out beside a low-lying meadow. The girl spurred abreast Benton and they crossed the meadow at a canter and entered a thicket of willows. Beyond that they halted. The Benton clearing lay to the fore, buildings bathed by the midmorning sun. One cloud sailed overhead like a fleecy pillow, and the dun distances of the prairie ran into a blue remoteness that had no definite ending. Benton's eyes struck all angles of the clearing and searched the sheds. He saw nothing, but he motioned to the girl. "Stay here till I go see if we've got visitors." Then he raced across the open and turned the far side of the main house. There were no ponies standing about. Dismounting, he went inside the house and explored it top and bottom. Somebody, he surmised, had been here recently; the kitchen stove was warm and a tin can held a brackish mixture of coffee.

Satisfied, he went out and signaled to the willow thicket. The girl came up.

"My dad," mused Benton, "had an idea of being a permanent citizen. He built this place to last. Even now, idle for so many years, it's still sound. A little repairing would make it snug and comfortable."

"Why was it your mother never sold it?"

"I don't know," mused Benton. "She never intended to come back and wouldn't stand for my coming back. But she paid taxes right along—and refused half a dozen offers. I think it was a memory she wanted to keep." An edge came to his talk. "And all the scoundrels in this country have stripped it. There'll be no more of that."

"I wish," said Rae, "I could be sure."

"We'll soon know," Benton murmured. "Like the place?"

"Another time," she answered very quietly, "I'll tell you about that. But I'm not going to hope too much, Jim. When I hope for a thing I lose it. So I'll not even dare to think of staying here—not until the fight is over."

"Won't be long," said Benton with the same slow doggedness of manner.

"It isn't too late yet to run," she put in, worry printed across her clear face.

"If I've got to leave here," said Benton stubbornly, "it will be feet first. This is my last stand."

Once again she shrugged her shoulders. And smiling a little at him, she went inside. He stood there for some time, listening to her feet roaming from one room to another. She called back once. "Somebody should be whipped for what's been done to these fine old walls." Hearing the anger in that comment, Benton grinned slowly and

120

strolled into the yard. About a hundred yards from the house he stopped to study its outline.

There was a strange feeling in him. He was sure of nothing. He had been knocked about, betrayed, and shot at until all his thoughts were cautious and trimmed to each short day. Permanence was something he had never known. Safety had always depended on his own vigilance, his own keen perception. And so, with his feet planted on soil that belonged to him, that strange, unusual feeling grew stronger and stronger. It was as if he put his roots down like some thirsty plant seeking water. Throughout his riding years he had been a restless hand, forever wanting something beyond the next hill. Well, this was the end of the journey—this was what he had been hunting for. This was home.

It astonished him that the pull of this benchland ranch was so strong. But there could be no question of it. Even now his eyes sought out those places familiar to him as a youngster. In those willows he had played hunter; in that farthest shed he had built his first figure-four trap—

There was a sound—a small, quick sound from the house. Looking about he found the girl standing at a second-story window. Her hand pointed, not at him, but to the north in the direction of the willows. Instantly on the alert, he turned, and his racing glance caught a slow weaving of the brush over there.

For a moment he stood still, realizing the target he made. The line of willows was five hundred feet away, admirable shelter. And it was more than possible that he was faced with several men instead of one. Considering that, he immediately guessed that he was not engaged with any part of the Blackrock posse. Those men would not be hiding in the brush. It was with Wolfert's partisans he had to deal. Eyeing the willow edges, he discovered no other point of activity; meanwhile the movement at the first discovered point ceased. One man, then. And this man crouched for a sure aim. That meant a rifle—no revolver could effectively reach a target at such a distance. Very slowly wheeling, Benton idled toward the house with an exaggerated show of indifference.

Between himself and the house stood a pump and a water trough. This was the shelter he wanted against that threatening gun, and as inconspicuously as he could make it he slightly shifted his march to come behind the heavy planks of the trough. Meanwhile his striding covered distance. He was within six good paces of the trough, all nerves tightened expectantly for the beat of the hidden weapon. The sun turned hot and the full bright light created a glare along the hard earth. He said slowly to himself: "He'll fire before I reach protection. But if he misses I'll get there ahead of the second shot." Then, feeling that he had played the moments for all that they were worth, he made one great forward lunge.

His leap broke the intolerable strain of waiting. A spanging echo filled the clearing and the rifle shell plucked the air hungrily behind him. After that he dived for the trough and rolled behind it; and then the marksman opened up with an angry abandon. Lead began to cut into the planks, making dull reverberations. Jets of dust leaped like snake heads at the exact meeting point of trough corner and ground. Tallying the shots with a cold methodicalness, Benton heard silence rush in. But he held his place, waiting for one more explosion. He knew that trick. Yet as the seconds ticked on he grew impatient of his sightless position and decided on another old trick. He took his hat and pushed it slowly beyond the end of the planks. Instantly afterwards it was whipped from his hand and went rolling away.

This was the break he waited for. A longer interval would follow before the marksman could get his fresh load into the rifle. Pulling himself erect, Benton left the trough on the run, aiming for the house. An enormous bellow drove from the brush; swinging his glance to the willows he saw Hale Wolfert smash out of them and appear in the open. Wolfert lifted his rifle and threw it away. He reached for his revolver, came directly on for a matter of a hundred feet, and then wheeled. A little later he vanished behind the house.

"Damn fool," said Benton to himself. "He threw off his advantage when he dropped the rifle. What's the matter with the man?" But as he asked the question, he thought he knew the answer. Wolfert had missed once, and he was too proud a man to continue a long-range battle. Utterly sure of his own power, he now elected to close in and end the debate with the revolver.

Benton considered this as he swept along the porch of the house and reached the open yard beyond. Wolfert appeared at about the same time, not farther than two hundred yards off. He saw Benton as Benton saw him. Instantly he turned from his direct charge, passed on to an adjacent wagon shed, and got out of sight once more. Not much afraid of a direct hit at such a distance, Benton continued his parallel course, and flanked a small smokehouse. Pacing back from it so that he might catch Wolfert's next dash either to left or right, he waited.

He had a very brief wait. Wolfert appeared on the left of the wagon shed. He saw Benton stationed there by the smokehouse and started forward rapidly. The next moment, however, he came to a halt and threw back those great shoulders that seemed to press down on the rest of his heavy body. Sunlight glistened on the dark cheeks, strengthened the formidable and brutally bold face. Mouth and nose showed a sudden, hawklike curve. In that brief pause Benton remembered his very first impression of Wolfert. The man was a killer born. Entirely ruthless and unforgiving.

"Benton," called Wolfert, "let's do no more dodgin'. I'm comin' straight at you."

"Come on," said Benton.

Wolfert held his peace briefly, looking all about. "If you've got any guts," he announced, "you'll stand your ground and settle this now."

"I'll be waiting."

"All right!" yelled Wolfert. "You're the man that's busted up these hills! Now, by God, I'll make no more mistakes!"

He lifted the gun and plunged on with his head half lowered, a flash of odd inflamed light shining from the half-closed eyes. The hot, dusty two hundred yards became a hundred and fifty. Benton stood quite still, small and stray impressions registering in a mind otherwise coldly concentrated. Somewhere behind Wolfert—somewhere over by the willows—was the sound of horses solidly pacing out of the hills. Wolfert's feet struck the earth soundly—all the magnificent muscles of his body swelled against the tight clothing. His jaw was thrown forward, and along the sides of the short, bull neck long ligaments made white and taut lines. Even then Benton felt a swift admiration for this bulky, conscienceless fighter. He had no fear. Wrong as he was and vicious as he was, Wolfert played out his part without weakening. In a world full of uncertainty it was actually good to find one lone hand who kept on as he had begun —no matter what evil stood behind that changeless energy. Benton lifted his gun, seeing more clearly than anything else the big checks on Wolfert's shirt. One of these checks seemed broader and brighter than the others. At a hundred yards Wolfert lifted his head and began to fire, not at all checking his pace.

Unconcious of it, Benton winced as the first slug went beside him. But he was still waiting for the interval to narrow, thinking now of nothing but one shot—only one shot—accurately placed. He felt Wolfert's second bullet hit at his feet. Wolfert cried an unmeaning phrase as he rushed on, tilting his gun higher. Benton shifted slightly in his tracks, pulled his weapon to the level of his eyes—and fired.

It was a direct hit and it jarred Wolfert out of his forward advance, having the effect of a solid blow. The man straightened and stiffened; and across the brutally stamped visage passed the strange and astonished and fearing suspicion that was a sure forecast of his fate. Benton made no attempt to try another aim. He knew. He had seen that expression before on the cheeks of men just before they died in violence. The sound of horses welled across the meadow, and rather faintly he got the back and forth calling of many men. But it was of no importance at this moment. Wolfert shook his shoulders. His gun slipped out of relaxing fingers. He issued a strangled cough, fear leaping out of his eyes. And then, struggling against it, he fell loosely to the ground. Benton pivoted away, wishing to see no more. Lifting his eyes, he found the meadow full of riders. A group of four circled the house and charged toward him. All of them covered him with their guns.

"If it's Wolfert you want, Sheriff," he said calmly, "you're too late."

There was no doubt about the sheriff. The man was furious, his face recognizable anywhere. Lean as rawhide, beyond middle-age, he sat loosely in the saddle and looked curiously down. A white cavalry mustache covered a white and rather grim mouth. Indigo blue eyes passed to the dead Wolfert and came back to center on Benton.

"You're Reno?"

"I used to travel under that name. It's no good now. I'm Hi Benton's son, back home."

"So," said the sheriff interestedly. He bent forward in the saddle, more clearly inspecting Benton. "You were little Jim Benton?" All the Blackrock riders were circled around Benton—dusty and jaded men in scowling humor. Rae McMurtree ran from the house and came across. She passed between the horses and stood beside Jim Benton, silently defiant. It was the habit of years—this instant antagonism to the riders of the flats—and she could not break it now.

"You've run me a merry chase, Jim," said the sheriff. "You know I want you, don't you?"

"You've got a warrant sworn by Dave LaTouche from over Shell River way?"

"Yeah," said the sheriff. "Chargin' you with cattle stealin'. Sorry. Get your horse."

"The warrant is no good," explained Benton gently. He reached into his pocket. The motion brought the trained guns quickly down on him, but he smiled and drew out a folded bit of paper. He walked over and handed it up to the sheriff. "The deal was framed. This is from LaTouche, to explain."

The sheriff unfolded and read the note. He looked up, coldly angry. "I don't get this. You and LaTouche frame a deal. LaTouche swears out a warrant and I spend my time chasin' you all over the flats. And here LaTouche says it don't mean anything. I want some clear talk on this."

"Here's your answer," said Benton, indicating the ranch. "I wanted to come back. My idea was to find the fellow that killed my dad. Well, how was I going to get into this country? If I rode into Blackrock as an ordinary hand I'd be suspected of something right away. Those fellows are always looking for the joker. Only way I could rig it was to come in all lathered, you on my trail. It made me out a crooked customer and it explained me. That's what Blackrock needed—an explanation."

"And supposin'," said the sheriff, "I'd got you?"

"Had to take the chance," Benton drawled. "It worked, didn't it? I got in. I found the man that killed my dad. I'm back on the ranch."

"Who killed Hi?" inquired the sheriff, bending still farther forward.

"One of two men. Both of them are dead—both bad enough to have done the trick and probably working together on that deal. Vilas and Wolfert."

The sheriff sat back, deeply thoughtful. His head nodded slightly as if Benton's talk satisfied him in some long suspended judgment. He had a reputation for taciturnity and quick action; and now he justified the reputation by reaching into his pocket and throwing a long-folded sheet to the ground. It was, Benton saw, an arrest warrant. "Burn it up and consider the story finished." Then he said slowly, evenly, "The hills are pretty clear of trouble. Are you fixin' to stay here?"

"I'm back for good," Benton stated. "This is the end of the road for me."

"As for the girl—"

"This McMurtree stays too, Sheriff. We'll run the hills together."

The sheriff turned to his nearest man. "Put Wolfert in a saddle. We'll take that chore off Benton's hands." Looking back to the girl, he raised his hat and bowed with a rather formal courtesy. "I'm glad to see it come out this way. Always admired you, Rae. Always had a sneaking respect for your dad. He's restin'—as we all will some day. Knowin' him, I'd say he was satisfied with the end. For you, life is only beginning. Benton, I consider you lucky. Good luck. Turn about, boys. We're through here."

They collected and cantered away, bearing Wolfert with them, and they went down the long undulating slopes of the bench. The girl looked up to Benton, speaking quietly.

"I can answer the question now, Jim. I love this place—and I'll try to make a home of it you'll want."

"The world is all before us," drawled Benton, sweeping the distant blue of the horizon with his hand.

The girl smiled a little and put her hand on his arm, possessively. "Come. We must start out right. You and I are going to walk through the front door of that house together, Jim. There's a happy omen in that."

He started to speak, but she shook her head. "Wait till we are inside. We'll christen the place then with what you want to tell me—and what I want to hear."

Big Bestsellers from SIGNET

- [ ] **'SALEM'S LOT** by Stephen King. (#J7112—$1.95)
- [ ] **CARRIE** by Stephen King. (#J7169—$1.95)
- [ ] **FATU-HIVA: Back to Nature** by Thor Heyerdahl. (#J7113—$1.95)
- [ ] **CBS: Reflections in a Bloodshot Eye** by Robert Metz. (#E7115—$2.25)
- [ ] **THE DOMINO PRINCIPLE** by Adam Kennedy. (#J7058—$1.95)
- [ ] **IF YOU COULD SEE WHAT I HEAR** by Tom Sullivan and Derek Gill. (#W7061—$1.50)
- [ ] **THE PRACTICE OF PLEASURE** by Michael Harris. (#E7059—$1.75)
- [ ] **ENGAGEMENT** by Eloise Weld. (#E7060—$1.75)
- [ ] **FOR THE DEFENSE** by F. Lee Bailey. (#J7022—$1.95)
- [ ] **THE SAMURAI** by George Macbeth. (#J7021—$1.95)
- [ ] **PLAYING AROUND** by Linda Wolfe. (#J7024—$1.95)
- [ ] **DRAGONS AT THE GATE** by Robert Duncan. (#J6984—$1.95)
- [ ] **WHERE HAVE YOU GONE JOE DI MAGGIO?** by Maury Allen. (#W6986—$1.50)
- [ ] **KATE: The Life of Katharine Hepburn** by Charles Higham. (#J6944—$1.95)
- [ ] **MISSION TO MALASPIGA** by Evelyn Anthony. (#E6706—$1.75)

THE NEW AMERICAN LIBRARY, INC.,
P.O. Box 999, Bergenfield, New Jersey 07621

Please send me the SIGNET BOOKS I have checked above. I am enclosing $_____(check or money order—no currency or C.O.D.'s). Please include the list price plus 35¢ a copy to cover handling and mailing costs. (Prices and numbers are subject to change without notice.)

Name_____

Address_____

City_____State_____Zip Code_____
Allow at least 4 weeks for delivery